MICHAEL

MICHAEL

A Novel

Joseph Goebbels

TRANSLATED FROM THE GERMAN
BY JOACHIM NEUGROSCHEL

AMOK PRESS
New York

Library of Congress Cataloging-in-Publication Data

Goebbels, Joseph, 1897–1945.
  Michael : a novel.

    1. Germany--History--1918-1933--Fiction.   I. Title.
PT2613.O19M513 1987   833'.913   87-11488
ISBN 0-941693-00-7

Interior design: Laura Lindgren

First Edition
10 9 8 7 6 5 4 3 2 1

PREFACE

Michael: Ein deutsches Schicksal in Tagebuchblättern
(*Michael: Pages From a German Destiny*—in this edition
shortened to *Michael*) is surmised by Goebbels' biographer,
Helmut Heiber, to have been written in 1923. It took until 1929,
when Goebbels found relative prominence as editor of *National
Socialist Letters* and *Völkische Freiheit*, to find *Michael* a
publisher, but by the end of the second world war, it had gone
through seventeen editions.

The year 1923 also marked the death of Goebbels' close
friend, Richard Flisges, to whom *Michael* is dedicated. Flisges
expressed anarchist, pacifist and Socialist views, and introduced
Goebbels to Marx, Engels, Lenin, and Dostoyevsky. Many
aspects of Flisges' life, most notably his exploits as soldier and
miner, were integrated into the composite that comprised the
portrait of *Michael*'s protagonist. Goebbels' own life completes
that portrait.

It must be remembered that socialism comprised half the formula of National Socialism. The "placid burghers" (Goebbels'
phrase) were attacked as being threats to nationalist integrity
with the same ferocity reserved for the Jews. Some of the most
interesting pages of *Michael* find its hero grappling in a
love/hate relationship with the purer products of the Slavic
soul. The Slavs are ultimately rejected by Goebbels' protagonist, of course, but at the same time are accorded the
respect of intellectual equals.

Writes George L. Mosse in *Nazi Culture*, "*Michael* reflects the
greater social emphasis of the future propaganda minister, the
socialism of National Socialism." Indeed, the last third of
Michael is taken up with its hero's efforts on behalf of his fellow
workers, who neither understand Michael nor want his help until it is too late. Goebbels' brand of socialism shuns Debsian
utopias or Leninist doctrines of "dictatorship of the proletariat."
Michael's God is a "God of strength. He does not like incense
fumes and the dishonoring crawl of the throng."

Much of what later comprised Nazi cultural ideology makes
an early appearance in *Michael*. Its hero is a perfectly balanced
Nazi renaissance man: soldier, worker, lover, *Völkische*

philosopher, poet, and scholar who finally rejects the sickliness of intellect for the sturdier virtues of action-oriented instinct. Encompassed within its pages are discussions of the degeneration of liberalism; the delights of nature; Judaism; expressionism; the true nature of Christ ("harsh and relentless"); love; Van Gogh; nihilism; the role of women; faith; Goethe; the virtues of work; and, significantly, Nietzsche. (*Michael* ends with a quote from *Thus Spake Zarathustra*). *Michael* can be seen as a distillation of National Socialist theology, a blueprint of its then-present and future concerns.

There is controversy over Goebbels' claims of early involvement with the Nationalsozialistische Deutsche Arbeite Partei, though circumstantial evidence supports the theory that Goebbels first heard Hitler speak in 1921 while a student at Munich University. An original holographic manuscript for *Michael* no longer exists, and so it is impossible to determine whether a significant scene in the novel was added for the 1929 edition, in which he attends a meeting where a seeming prototype of Hitler speaks: "Two glowing eyes flash lightning. . . . His fists are clenched . . . word upon word, sentence upon sentence boom like the Last Judgment. . . . I shout, 'Hurray!' No one is surprised. The man on the podium gazes at me for a moment. Those blue eyes strike me like flaming rays. . . . I am reborn as of that moment."

What might seem today an almost naive romanticism in *Michael* jars with contemporary portraits of a cynical and calculating propaganda minister. The topic for Goebbels' Ph.D. thesis, *Wilhelm Schuetz: A Contribution to the History of the Romantic Theater*, as well as his lyric poems and plays which have such titles as *Deep in Dreams I Wandered the Dark Wood*, *Those Who Are Loved by the Sun*, *The Wanderer*, *The People's Death Song*, reveal an intoxication with the romantic theme.

In its structure, *Michael* recalls the style of those other, more familiar Goebbels documents, his late diaries. Written while Goebbels was in his early twenties, and devised as a work of fiction, *Michael* detours into many metaphysical plaints and raptures, but all the characteristic Goebbelsian traits found in his diaries are present. A penchant for the catchy aphorism, clipped ejaculatory rhythms and opinionated effrontery appear both in

Michael as well as all the published diaries. Helmut Heiber asserts that *Michael* is largely drawn from Goebbels' diaries of 1919 and 1920 (they no longer exist) while he was a student in Freiburg and Munich. If this is true, we can divine from the fictional *Michael* Goebbels' factual sense of personal destiny; his diaries were not designed to belong under lock and key, but to the open book of history while their protagonist burst upon the world stage.

Adam Parfrey

MICHAEL

DEDICATION

1918

You stood, with your shot, shattered arm in a sling, the gray helmet on your battered head, your chest covered with iron crosses, you stood in front of placid burghers, taking the oral examination for your high-school degree. Because you did not know a few figures, they decreed that you should not pass.

Our answer was: Revolution!

1920

The two of us were about to surrender to a mental breakdown. But we straightened up with one another's help and we barely stumbled.

My answer was: Defiance!

1923

You challenged your destiny to a duel. All or nothing! But it was still too early. That was why you fell victim.

Your answer was: Death!

1927

I stood at your grave; a quiet, green mound lay in the glowing sunshine. And it preached ephemeralness.

My answer was: Resurrection.

I dedicate this book to the memory of my friend

RICHARD FLISGES

who, on July 19, 1923, in a mine near Schliersee, died a difficult death as a brave warrior of labor.

FOREWORD

This is the deepest blessing of this life: The forces of a young existence ascend from its mysterious depths in an everlasting exchange. Crisis is the path to happiness. Decay and disintegration do not spell doom, but ascent and beginning. The powerful forces of a new creation operate in the hush beyond the noise of the day.

Youth today is more alive than ever before. Youth believes. In what? That is the gist of the struggle. Seeds of new forms of existence sprout from youth, subdued but striving towards the light.

Youth is always right in any conflict with old age.

Hearts that delight in the future burn and blaze with the will to create, to live, to take form. Millions painfully wait for the day. In the garrets of tenements, in the barns of day laborers and the camps of migrants, filled with cold, hunger, and spiritual torment, the hope and symbol of a different time are taking shape. Faith, struggle, and work are the virtues that unite the German youth of today in its Faustian urge to create.

We are gradually coming together; the spirit of resurrection, the release from the self, the movement towards the Thou, the brother, the nation is a bridge from here to there.

We look towards the day that will bring the storm wind. At the right moment, we will have the courage to concentrate our will and do our deed for the Fatherland. We want life: That is why we shall win life.

Michael's diary is a monument to German fervor and devotion, a diary that wants to shake and comfort. Its modest, silent mirror reflects all the forces that are shaping us young people into a thought today and a power tomorrow. That is why Michael's life and death are more than mere chance and blind destiny. They are a sign of the times and a symbol of the future.

A life of service and labor and a death for the formation of a coming nation: That is the most comforting thing we can see on earth.

Express Train, 2 May

The thoroughbred stallion is no longer snorting under my thighs, I am no longer sitting on cannon benches, nor am I trudging through the loamy mire of neglected trenches. Long, long ago, I was plodding across the vast Russian steppe or through a bleak and battered French countryside. Those days are gone forever!

I am slowly recovering. I rise like a phoenix from the ashes of war and destruction.

Peace!

This word is like balm on a wound that still trembles and bleeds. I feel as if I could clutch the full goodness of this word with my hands.

When I look out the window, I see German countryside floating by: towns, villages, forests, fields. A silent path winds through brown farmland. Flowers bloom along the edges.

Children play in village streets.

Towering factory chimneys loom in the crystal air.

I pass vast green meadows. They glow in a thousand colors and lights. I open the window and breathe, breathe deep. Sunshine lies on German land.

This must have been how the Greeks greeted the sea.

Homeland! Germany!

A blossoming in the fields and gardens; intoxicating, extravagantly beautiful for eyes that have seen nothing but ruins and filth, blood and death for four years.

I am borne along like a floating island. Towards freedom!

I was in Frankfurt and I paid homage to the young Goethe. Today, he is still a leader in the battle of minds. A champion of every young will. Our mecca is not Weimar.

I have only one book in my pocket: *Faust*. I read the first part. I am too stupid for the second part.

Heidelberg! Nestled in a charming valley. The castle stands on the mountain. Students sing on the station platform.

The impatient wheels roll on again. On!

Hills become mountains! The land steams in the sun.

My eyes drink in God's beauty!

5 May

I now sit inside my own four walls, I am a student, free, my own lord and master. How often did I long for this in the din of battles.

I stroll through the streets and alleys as if I had been at home here for years. We learned this on the battlefield: to sit down and be here. The town is beautiful and agreeable. The people in this province have time. You hardly ever see anyone in a hurry. We are already deep in the south.

There are benches on Karlsplatz. They are always occupied, morning, noon, and night. I have never seen a bench that was not occupied.

The chestnut trees on the castle hill light their white candles. Whenever I have time (and when would I not have time), I stroll up the hill. The town lies below. The old houses cluster around the weathered cathedral like chicks around the broodhen. The sun glitters and flashes on the red roofs in the new part of town.

The countryside glows far and wide. The Vosges emerge hazily in the distance.

A year ago, somewhere around here, I stood in drumfire, and I had only one wish: End the torture, die, fall, be a hero, know nothing more.

And today I stand here and I want to clutch life with all the fibers of my being.

8 May

I live in the last house at the edge of town. My window faces a blossoming garden.

The sun shines into my room almost all day long. The sky over this town is a southern, deep blue.

When I walk to the university, I pass through these clean streets, which exist only in Germany. Canals run along the sidewalks, carrying sparkling spring water. Flocks of children wade knee-deep in the water, playing pranks on the passersby.

I live in the lap of luxury!

In the evening, I walk home through narrow, deserted streets, past the cathedral. Sometimes, I hear only my own footsteps. The evening air caresses my face. When I stand still, I hear a fountain murmuring and splashing somewhere.

A nightly dialogue beyond human beings.

At the open window:
  A final breath
  Of weary birdsong
  And fragrant lilac
  Is wafted by the evening wind
  Into my room.
  I cannot sleep!

12 May

I run into my high school friend Richard. (We also saw each other in the army a couple of times.) How glad we are to meet again! He asks me what I am studying.

What *am* I studying?

Everything and nothing. I am too lazy and I think I am too stupid to specialize in anything.

I want to become a man! I want to have a profile.

Personality! The road to the new German!

Style is everything! Style is harmony between law and expression. If you want to have style, you must have both law and expression.

Thus, style is nothing but doing, bringing forth, suffering, and shaping everything according to your own law, and doing all these things as a matter of course.

The stress is on "matter of course."

If there is no fire burning in you, how can you ignite!

16 May

Richard visits me in the evening. We sit in the garden and talk until late at night. He is intelligent and sensible, and, above all, he knows a great deal.

We exchange memories from our earliest childhood. I can see the village, the garden, my home. Through an open window, I hear my mother bustling about in the kitchen.

Mother!

One need have nothing—only a mother.

If a mother is not everything to her children—a friend, teacher, confidant, a source of joy and solid pride, a spur, a restraint, an accuser, a conciliator, a judge, and a forgiver—that mother has obviously missed her calling.

My mother is a divine spendthrift: in everything, from money to the pure goodness of her heart.

She gives whatever she has and often far more.

Only a mother has the true instinct for her children.

17 May

I have given a great deal of thought to what it is that makes me drink life to its fullest and so rashly at that.

I stand with both feet on the hard soil of my homeland. I am surrounded by the aroma of the earth. Farmer's blood rises in me, slow and healthy.

Richard calls me a man of existence.

I walk alone, climbing the narrow paths of the castle hill, breathing the warm fragrance of a May night charged with blossoms.

I rise with the sun, and I go to rest with the stars. I sleep four hours and I am refreshed and exhilarated.

18 May

In the afternoon, I sit in the old, silent, cemetery. In front of me, a fountain sprays its fine rain into the hot air. Chestnut trees form a roof overhead. The ivy modestly curls around the gravestones in the green webs.

The singing of blackbirds! Nothing else troubles the sleep of the dead.

A bee hums.

I read Nietzsche's *Afternoon Worship* from *Zarathustra*.

Still. . . . Still. . . .

Everything dissolves in the cosmos. Pan! . . .

20 May

In the classrooms of the university, there is a great deal of writing, even more talking, and, it seems to me, awfully little learning. You always find a certain type of eager beaver here. Pale faces, intelligentsia glasses, fountain pens, and thick brief-cases full of books and notebooks. That is all.

The future leaders of the nation!

And women, oh me, oh my! And the bluestockings are the most bearable ones.

I look for the teacher who is simple enough to be big and big enough to be simple.

Specialization encourages arrogance and narrow-mindedness. It usually wrecks common sense.

Intellect is a danger to the development of the character.

We are not on earth to stuff our skulls with knowledge. It is all so peripheral if it has no relationship to life. We have to fulfill our destinies and educate real men; that should be the task of the universities.

We can only make ourselves into what God has put into us.

Hence, Goethe is the greatest man because he went beyond the limits of German consciousness. But it would be wrong to try and imitate him. All the much-preached emulation of Goethe is nonsense, the crazy ideas of empty, overeducated minds.

Quod licet Iovi, non licet bovi!

And that is what life is like: If Herr Meyer knows *Faust* by heart, he is merely demonstrating that he has a good memory. Why does he not tackle the logarithm table!

22 May

The old privy councilor talks about the homeland of the first Teutons. I seldom attend his course. But how often have I heard him say that our forebears lived on the lower Danube and the coast of the Black Sea. A young woman sits right in front of me: a beautiful woman! Blondish-brown hair, silky soft, in a heavy knot on the back of that wonderful neck. Her neck is hewn out of pale yellow marble. She peers dreamily out the window, through which a playful sunbeam steals in, softly, almost timidly. I see her fine profile: a cleanly curving brow, with a few stray curls above it, a long, sharp, somewhat broad nose, and, underneath, a soft, visionary mouth.

As I gaze at her, she suddenly turns around to me, and I look into a pair of large, grayish-green enigmas. Now, all at once, she sits still and proper, she seems to be listening attentively to the weary words of the old teacher, and she acts as if she is studiously taking notes. The prying sunbeam comes hippity-hopping through the window, quivering over the seats, all of which are occupied; it finally pauses in her blondish-brown hair.

Her hair glows like soft, golden silk slipping through your fingers in light.

It is evening. I stand at the window, Richard sits lecturing in my large armchair. He talks about Marxism. How rationalistic it all is. Marxism is a doctrine of money and stomachs. It assumes that a living human being is a machine. That is why Marxism is wrong, alien to life, an intellectual construction, not organic. Logical in theory, but illogical in practice.

How little is solved by it! The spirit of breadth and not of depth. And what does Marxism have to do with our torment?

What happens when I turn the conversation to women? Richard talks about them too, as usual, in an intelligent and thorough way.

Woman exists. Man is awake.

Man is the organizer, woman the director of life.

Man supplies the line, woman the color.

Why am I not keeping pace with my thoughts today? I swim in a sea of vague wishes and desires.

Now I am alone. I stand at the window, and above me, a cloudless sky arches in its starry vastness. The wind softly caresses the trees in the garden below.

The full hour blesses me!

Night folds trembling hands
Over the weary world.
The moon rises shiny
From the pale blueness.
My thoughts soar
Like lonesome swans
To the stars.

A sunbeam on a woman's blondish-brown hair. . . .

23 May
I sit next to her in class. She is bashful and sedulously writes in her notebook that the homeland of the original Teutons was probably the lower Danube and goodness knows where else. I hear her breathe faster, I feel the warmth of her body, and I inhale the fresh scent of her hair. Her hand rests casually, almost next to mine. It is long, narrow, and as white as newly fallen snow.

The bell rings—and, fool that I am, I grab my belongings and stalk away.

It is sunny outside. I sit on the terrace and watch the hustle and bustle of the academics, their laughter, their jokes. I catch fragments of conversations: duels, heavy sabers, phenomenology, transcendency, historically proven. . . .

24 May
Hertha Holk: I read the name in her notebook. How much closer just a name brings us. We are no longer strangers even though we have not exchanged a single word.

I read Goethe's *Wilhelm Meister*. This epic is almost too round and too vast for us; it has too few corners.
At the Goethe House in Frankfurt, a guide and I were standing on the stairway, and he showed me the courtyard in which little Wolfgang used to play with his sister. I almost had tears in my eyes.

A portrait of Lotte Buff hangs upstairs in his room. After his period in Wetzlar, he became an attorney in Frankfurt, and every afternoon when he came home from the office, he would storm up the stairs and into his room, where he doffed his hat to the portrait and said, "Hello, Lotte!"

That was the Goethe whom we young people love. The privy councilor is sometimes unbearable.

Character is part of art. Writing beautiful poems is not consistent with being an unbearable person.

Perhaps that is why Schiller rather than Goethe became the poet of the German people.

And perhaps that is why we love Beethoven's Ninth Symphony more than Mozart's *The Magic Flute*.

Art is not just ability, it is also struggle. Titans, not Olympians, are the guides for a struggling generation.

No miracles happen now because we see no miracles now.

A miracle, in its innermost essence, is poetry; it can be likened to the folk song.

A thing is only what you make of it; that includes you too.

I am running out of money; money is filth, but filth is not money.

25 May

I enter the lecture hall. She blushes and grows confused. I sit down two seats behind her.

How endless an hour can be!

30 May

Hertha Holk and I are good friends.

Oh, this world is beautiful because of you!

Loving another human being brings us closer to God.

That is not true: Today's youth is not against God, we are only against his cowardly religious menials, who try to commercialize him as they do everything else.

We have to square off against them if we want to square ourselves with God.

31 May

Today is a clean, lovely Saturday morning. I stroll over to the cathedral. There are beautiful Black Forest women there, selling flowers.

What a splendidly colorful scene: the cathedral looming in the background, earnest and solemn, reddish-brown; and in front of it, flower-stands and women in black dresses and red kerchiefs.

At one stand, I see Hertha Holk buying flowers. She chats with the old market woman. She says something, the old woman laughs—and then both of them laugh.

Now she buys three long-stemmed red carnations. Then she sees me, acts extremely confused for a moment, and then comes toward me, smiling in embarrassment.

The park around Colombi Castle is full of the peace and quiet of the morning. No one strays here this early.

The sunlight moves, broad and easy, across the paths. A bird sings wearily in the trees. We sit here until noon.

She tells me about her home, about the land of the red earth, where people labor furiously, where chimneys fume and flues smoke, she tells me about her father, who died when she was only eight, about her mother, who, without giving it a second thought, took the father's place and lived on for the children.

A great, courageous woman, who takes everything as it is.

How greatly you resemble your mother, Hertha Holk!

"What am I majoring in? The question would be more fitting for you, since law and art go together like oil and water."

She laughs: "Law as my profession and art for fun."

"Profession—that sounds so discordant on your lips."

A pause!

"What about you?"

"I really don't know yet. Today, there is only one calling for a young German: To stand up for the Fatherland. We did it unprotestingly for four years. It is hard giving it up. That is one of the worst conflicts in the generation of soldiers. There is too great a leap from the trench to the lecture hall."

"You're not working very much?"

"Not in classes, to be sure! But I think one can learn in other places too. Best of all with the simplest things. Life itself is not complicated. We simply make it complicated. If you keep your eyes open, you can see it through.

"We make the simplest issues difficult and then brood ourselves sick about them."

"You write poetry, don't you?"

"What makes you think so?"

"Just a thought. It would suit you."

"Well I do. Yes! Sometimes! I don't like 'professional' poets, or rather, 'writers.' A real poet is something like an amateur photographer of life. After all, a poem is nothing but a snapshot from an artistic soul. Art is an expression of feeling. The artist differs from the non-artist in his ability to express what he feels. In some form or other. One artist does it in a painting, another in clay, a third in words, and a fourth in marble—or even in historical forms. The statesman is also an artist. For him, the nation is exactly what the stone is for the sculptor. Führer and masses, that is as little of a problem as, say, painter and color.

"Politics is the fine art of the state, just as painting is the fine art of color. That is why politics without the people, or actually against the people, is a contradiction in terms. Forming the masses into a nation, and a nation into a state—that has always been the deepest goal of true politics. Politics cannot possibly spoil one's character. The only people who say it can are the ones who spoil politics with their own bad characters."

"What about today?"

"Ah, today! That's not politics that they're pursuing up there. They are merely doing their own business with the people's money. Our so-called politics has no intrinsic relationship to the people. And that is why we will eventually go under."

"But things are better now, aren't they?"

"Better? Oh, no, we've become worse. We no longer have any sense of honor and duty. Food is the only issue. But anyone who sells his honor will soon lose his food. That is a late, but all the crueler vengeance of history."

"You write poetry and you pursue politics?"

"Pursue politics? That is a silly question. Politics is something we pursue as a matter of course. Every father who brings children into the world is pursuing politics. Every mother who turns her boys into men is a political being.

"People have turned politics into a vocation—as though politics were something one could learn. How erroneous! Moreover, every army private who did his duty uncomplainingly on the battlefield knew more about the profession of politics and practiced it more effectively than the parliamentary chatterboxes who sat in government offices and gave speeches."

"You're very harsh in your judgment!"

"One can't be harsh enough. If a man wants to master life, he must deal with it the way life deals with him. Life, too, is harsh."

"War is terrible."

"That means nothing. No sensible human being has ever doubted it. But trying to abolish war would be like trying to keep mothers from having children. This, too, is terrible. Everything about life is terrible.

"One can only resort to protective measures against war: That means enabling a nation to defend itself so that no one else would care to rob it of its right to live."

"Both a poet and a soldier live inside you. Do you also play music?"

"A little."

"Would you feel like playing something for me tomorrow afternoon?"

"I would like that very much."

We separated. It was noon. The sun was glowing on the grayish-white asphalt.

As I left, Hertha Holk gave me one of her carnations. She blushed and was suddenly very confused. She barely shook my hand, nodded in great embarrassment, and vanished around the next corner.

The artist can be compared to God. Both give form to matter. The artist is a piece of God.

Let there be light! And there is light!

Is art cheerful? Sometimes it is difficult and almost unbearable.

Art must shake you and exalt you; it is a gain and a solace. It spares us nothing.

I do not hit upon thoughts; I am overcome by them, like the man from Jericho going to Jerusalem.

Times do not change, men change the times.

Men make history.

Am I in love with Hertha Holk?

I am almost frightened by the crudeness of the word "love."

She releases my thoughts, making them freer and more conscious.

Women inspire.

Three men sit together, bored. A woman joins them (she is not even beautiful) and the three men are transformed. They become scintillating—bright, witty, sparkling. Each tries to outdo the others.

A woman enters a man's existence like a magic wand.

A long-stemmed red carnation shines on my table.

Hertha Holk!

1 June

Hertha Holk sings Brahms's *Sapphic Ode* in a marvelous alto voice. Then I play Schubert's impromptus until late at night.

In conclusion, Hugo Wolf: "Thou Art Orplid My Land."

"Kings, who are thy servants, bow to thy divinity."

The whole *lied* climaxes in this great chord. The kings bow to the divinity.

I wander through the starry night for hours on end. Notes and harmonies echo within me.

Everything around me awakens like a new life.

Hertha Holk, I love you!!!

The night is my best friend. It calms the tempest in the soul and lets the guiding stars rise.

Day will soon dawn! And in me too!

I turn my little room into a royal castle and see the marble columns shine.

War is the simplest form of the affirmation of life.

A mother stakes her life, thus giving life to a child. A mere instant before death, a final will surges up in the old man and he cries: "I don't want to die!" Struggle when man comes upon this earth. Struggle when he leaves it, and in between there is an eternal war for a place at the trough.

I become aware of the profound blessing of ownership only when I have to keep defending my property against the envious. One appreciates only the things that one conquers or defends.

Peace, too, must be fought for, not with the palm frond but with the sword.

The worst crime that the saviors of the republic committed was to turn socialism into organized cowardice.

Everything with a human countenance is equal. That statement is made only by fools or by people pretending to be fools. The former because they believe it, the latter because they profit from it.

Nature herself is anti-democratic. Nowhere in the universe does she make any two living creatures alike.

Nature is the eternal, infallible teacher of life. One cannot outfox her. Sometimes she puts up with such attempts for a while, just for fun. But then she takes revenge, with punishments that are all the crueler.

Her forms may change, but never her contents.

The state is folkhood that has taken form.

Folkhood is the sum of all natural life-utterances of a nation. The state is nothing but the consciously organized protection of these life-utterances. The state without the nation or against the nation is the same as a suit without a man or a suit against a man; a contradiction in terms.

What does socialism have to do with the republic? There are

socialist monarchies and capitalist republics.

Being a socialist means subordinating the *I* to the *you*, sacrificing the individual personality to the totality. In its deepest sense, socialism is service. Renunciation of the individual and advancement for the whole society.

Frederick the Great was a socialist on the royal throne.

"I am the first servant in the state." A king's socialist statement!

Property is theft: That is what the mob says. To each his own: that is what the character says.

You all confuse capital and capitalism. Capitalism is abuse with the help of capital. Down with capital? No. Down with capitalism!

Credo, ergo sum!

One must weep with the clouds. Must one? I for my part have no intention of doing so.

If God created me in his own image, then I am a piece of him. God!

The greater and more towering I make God, the greater and more towering I am myself.

Inside me, everything hung still, like a clock pendulum that has been tied fast.

The clockwork has been wound, and the pendulum and the hands start to move.

Everything relaxes in me, and my thoughts become as light as wafting pollen.

3 June

Sunlight shines through my window. I stand and peer out into the crystal-clear morning. I let all my wishes and desires flutter down like leaves into the blossoming garden.

The instant you come to pick your roses, you find them. Take them and place them on your shimmering white table. They will be delightfully fragrant all morning.

8 June
Whitsuntide! All the fields are in blossom!
Hertha Holk is in Beuron!

What use is all the varnish of thought, when love over-comes a man?

10 June
Two hours stopover in Tuttlingen. I barely know how I started out.
I have to see Hertha Holk!

Beuron! Solitude! Cloistral hush!
The sun shines hard on the dusty highway. I have been sitting for a long time, waiting for Hertha Holk.
She does not come home from her walk until evening. She sees me. Disappointment, amazement, embarrassment, and then joy on her face, immense joy. We greet each other like old friends. After supper, we sit in a quiet nook by the church. We hear prayers and singing as though from afar. The monks pray-ing vespers. And then, stillness, wonderful stillness.
The sun has already set.
No sound can be heard far and wide. We remain silent, too.
I think of the red summer days at home. As a boy, I would run across the fields for hours to try to see the sunset up close.

Somewhere, a door is closed. A male voice, then a female voice. Children praying! Dear Jesus mine! Then stillness again. Wonderful stillness!
The night places its broad, black wings across the land.
"I sit here every evening, and feel as if I were finding a refuge from tempests."
A pause.
"Outside, we hurry after the day."
"And we cannot get away from it."
"And then we are suddenly amazed that the world is so solemn and still."
"We are poor, torn, tormented human beings. Time has

broken into our hearts."

"And yet we come closer to redemption."

"We have endured a great deal already. We will have to endure a lot more. Let us thank God that we are young."

We sit in silence. It is getting cool. Slowly we walk home.

"Good night, and sleep well."

After a pause:

"You gave me great joy today."

Then she vanishes upstairs.

I stand, gazing into the star-covered night. A window opens overhead. I almost sense someone breathing.

The night is so still.

A light burns somewhere. Now it goes out. The monastery lies beneath me like a gray mass. The church tower strikes two. I lie down across the bed, fully clothed.

> The night is here!
> I lie
> And dream
> With open eyes
> Into the dark distance.
> I greedily inhale an
> Intoxicating scent.
> Somewhere
> A nightingale sings.
> I wait, wait, wait.

Good night, Hertha Holk!

11 June

She is not allowed to enter the monastery. I walk with the guide, a father, through the long, white corridors. Small, delicate monastic paintings on the walls. Local art. Delightful lines, the colors somewhat stolid. A strange hobby!

Book after book in the library.

A father sits at his work. He does not even look up. His face is pale and narrow, with sharply notched lines.

I thank my guide. He shakes my hand. Praised be Jesus Christ!

It is a bright morning outside. Last night it rained, and now everything smells of freshness and blossoms.

Hertha Holk stands slender, in a white frock, at the monastery gate. A strange contrast!

We stroll out into the fields and sit on a mountain slope until noon, overlooking an entire valley.

I want to speak. She gazes at me, a quizzical gaze, beseeching, almost imploring. Be still! Not yet! I understand. We go home.

After lunch, I study the train schedule, and I leave at three p.m. She sees me off at the station.

As I leave, she gives me a small local painting, an *Ecce Homo*. Soft, lovely lines, clear and simple. It is like a talisman for me.

A last handshake, a last wave.

I see her for a long time from my train window, I watch her walking up the street, step by step, leisurely, lowering her head.

Fields on either side of the train, sheaves and flowers.

I feel as if I were being carried through a blossoming garden.

12 June

I am sitting at the tavern in Lindau, staring at the vast, glassy surface of Lake Constance.

I am thinking of Hertha Holk.

Then I stroll through the narrow alleys of the old, narrow rows of houses.

During lunch, I gaze across the lake. There are many people in the hotel. Women shriek, shout, laugh, and cackle. A Russian student sits at my table. He will be sailing with me to Meersburg.

Our ship leaves at three p.m.

13 June

Meersburg: I live in a small guesthouse right by the castle. This is where the great German poetess Annette von Droste-Hülshoff lived. I walk up the wide street to the cemetery. A small gravesite, surrounded by an iron lattice, a simple stone, overgrown with ivy. Here lies Germany's poetess. The words on the stone say:

Anna Elisabeth von Droste-Hülshoff
Glory be to the Lord

A bouquet of red roses lies on the grave.

The note says: "From vacationing students from Munich, in gratitude to the great poetess!"

I see her rooms in the castle. There is a lingering sense of austere virginity. On the balcony, I gaze across the lake, which now lies still, in the final rays of the sun. She must have stood here often, her eyes yearning for the white Swiss mountains.

Italy lies beyond them!

I rent a boat and glide slowly into the lake. The sun has set.
    I pull in
    The oars
    And glide endlessly,
    As if to an
    Eternal Shore.
    Moonlight flashes blue
    On my sail.
    My skiff glides
    Into a safe harbor.
    The waves
    Beat very softly
    Against my boat.
    Deepest stillness
    Surrounds me,
    And my soul
    Spans a golden bridge
    To a star.

14 June

I want to rest here for a few days. Every stone, every tree exhales calm and composure. I am comforted by the memory of a person who lived here and wrote poetry. I am content, happy.

I think of you joyfully, Hertha Holk!

I sit by the lake all morning, meditating about the deepest things. I converse with God.
I believe that ultimately truth will be stronger than lies.
In my best hours, I believe in myself.
It does not much matter what we believe, so long as we believe.

I am in the process of demolishing the old world of faith in me. I shall raze it totally. Then I shall build a new world. I shall begin at the bottom and erect piece by piece. I am doing so in difficult hours. I struggle with myself to find a new God.
I hear God in the rustling of the leaves. I see his presence in the everlasting change. I worship him in the morning, when the sun rises.

Man is good in God's eyes.
Man is will, and the will loves God.
My God is a god of strength. He does not like incense fumes and the dishonoring crawl of the throng.
I stand before him, my head raised proudly, as he created me, and I declare my faith in him, freely and joyfully.
A true German is a God-seeker all his life.
Poor is the man who is complete.

The Russian's name is Ivan Vienurovsky. He is studying philosophy in Munich. He lives next door to me in the guesthouse. We sit together and talk. He tells me about Russia. What a racial sense of nation; the Russians believe in their future.
He lends me Dostoyevsky's *The Idiot*. We go our separate ways late at night.
My window remains open. A linden tree arches outside, in front of the guesthouse. It thrusts its branches into my room. The moon shines through them, and onto my floor in pale

yellow spots.

Everyone has retired. Only two lovers sit down below, under the linden tree, chatting, tittering, laughing.

15 June

Hertha Holk writes to me:

> We will see each other in a few days, fortified, resolute, and with the courage to struggle. I miss you very much. Give my best to my fellow German, dear Anna Elisabeth von Droste-Hülshoff. Once again, I long to leave my peace and quiet and go out into the world. We human beings are homeless on earth since we never find peace anywhere.

> I have sought clarity and reflection here and found them. I have faith again. We young people shall not go under so long as we believe in our mission. Think of the deep meaning of the proverb: Faith alone makes us blessed.

I have placed a bouquet of wildflowers on Annette's grave.

It is a lovely Sunday. I am in the boat, rocking on the glassy surface of Lake Constance and reading Dostoyevsky's *The Idiot*.

Prince Myshkin is an unstable, unpredictable, ridiculous man, an idiot. But that is the way the Russians are, and that is their tragic grandeur.

Christianity is not a religion for the majority, much less for all. Cultivated by the few and translated into deeds, it is one of the most beautiful blossoms that the soul of a culture has ever borne.

Hotheaded, abrupt, direct, endlessly brooding, waiting, hoping, infinitely evil and infinitely good, filled with the deepest passions, kind and tender, fanatical in both lies and truth, young and callow, yet very profound, rich in joy, humor, pain and yearning: That is the Slavic soul; the soul of Russia.

Dostoyevsky soars from passion to passion, from problem to problem, from depth to depth. Irascible pain and irascible joy; people in distorted forms, unnaturalness and race, corruption, abyss and genius, madness and idiocy; pure and cerebrally clear as the sun, and ludicrously, pathologically misshapen: That is his opus.

A great racial soul in the cramps of birth and death. One is virtually at the bed of a sick man. One sniffs the air of crisis.

Dostoyevsky is several daring steps ahead of his time. One follows him, dizzy, fearful, unbelieving; but one follows him. He haunts you; you have to follow him.

Here we find everything: naturalism, expressionism, idealism, skepticism, and whatever other isms we can distill from him. Yet one cannot really talk about these things in connection with him. Dostoyevsky knows them only by name.

He describes what he sees, what his demon, his devil, burns into his brain and soul. He writes because in the nineteenth century that was one of the few possibilities of becoming something. Politics was in its embryonic stage. He writes because his love of Russia, his hatred of anything foreign, his hatred of the West, scorch his soul.

One must simply take him as unique. He comes from nowhere and belongs nowhere. And yet he always remains Russian.

His novels are grandiose ballads. What you find on the pages is ridiculous, petty, insignificant, sometimes meaningless. Everything is to be found between the lines.

One must divine, and grope for, the ultimate in him.

Tinsel, rubbish, and frippery, form and symbol—behind them, a national soul forging ahead.

Ivan Vienurovsky smiles when I say these things to him, the things I struggle to set down here. After all, Dostoyevsky is his profession of faith, his gospel.

"We believe in Dostoyevsky the way our fathers believed in Christ," he says.

The old, new Russia borders on the huge problem known as Europe. Russia is the past and perhaps also the future, but not the present. For the Russian present is mere lather over the heavy suds. The solution to Russia's great enigma is brooding in her earth. The ghost of Dostoyevsky, promising a great future, haunts the quiet, dreaming land. When Russia awakens, the world shall witness a national miracle.

A national miracle? Yes, that is what it will be. Political miracles occur only on the national scale. The international is, after all, merely a doctrine of the mind, against the blood. The miracle of a nation never lies in the brain, but only in the blood.

What the Russians call international is a mishmash of Jewish hair-splitting, cowardly and bloody terrorism, boundless endurance of the broad masses—thrust into the era of world politics by the overwhelming will of a single man: Lenin.

Without Lenin, there would be no Bolshevism.

Once again: Men make history. Even bad history.

The peasants have been freed in Russia. Have they? Yes, to an extent, because there was no other choice. But this is no Marxism.

"Property is theft!" says the upright fighter against the class system. Lenin gave land to every Russian peasant. Since then, a hundred million thieves have been living in Russia.

When Ivan Vienurovsky speaks, he becomes very tender and timid; but his words are haunted by a secret demon. We debate for hours on end.

16 June

Richard writes: "The world is nothing but a big theater: The good Lord is the producer, the kings, princes, statesmen, and capitalists are his directors, the poets and artists his lead players—and we are the extras."

Two fat high school teachers from the Rhineland have arrived in the guesthouse. Richard remarks spitefully that this type could only have been cultivated in Germany. This sounds embarrassing, and it is incorrect.

Granted, this type bears a great responsibility for our national misfortune, but such men do have their merits.

We Germans think too much. The German intellectual

philistine has killed our instinct for politics.

We are the most intelligent, but, alas, also the stupidest nation in the world.

Vienurovsky talks about the war and the Russian Revolution. He sounds tired, almost tormented, and at times he almost seems to be angry at me. But he is only expressing his anger at Russia.

I speak about the Germany of the future. He refuses to believe that we still have the will and strength for a renaissance of the German will for mind and power.

The Russian is being unfair to us. He has no reason for this.

And besides, foreigners do not see what lies under the surface in Germany. We young people are only a thought for now, but we are gradually ripening into action. Just give us time. We are not yet mature.

We young people are groping our way forwards. After the war, we were numb and paralyzed for a while. But everything is flowing again.

The great masses? Ah, they never foment. Revolutions (and what we are going through now is a vast cultural revolution) are always made by individuals. The masses are carried along.

Revolution is a creative act. It overcomes the final vestiges of collapsing eras and clears the way for the future.

The war was the beginning of our revolution; but it was not carried through. When the war ended, the revolution was adulterated, twisted, degraded, and that is why the younger generation has lost for the time being.

This is the crux: Labor is rebelling against money. The supporter of labor is the blood, the supporter of money is gold. The war was act one of the revolution of the twentieth century, in which labor is marching out against money. It is our job to win in the second or third act.

Revolutions create new men first, then new times.

An upheaval is initially impelled by a revolutionary type, not by social misery. The latter is an added factor. The revolutionary exploits it in order to achieve his power-political goals.

Men have to destroy if they want to create anew. One cannot liberate labor and yet spare money.

When the veterans came home from the Great War, they carried, on their rifles, the will for a new state. But beyond the borders, the profiteers had already turned the shards of the old Reich into a new hybrid. The warriors planted their bayonets in front of it as a defense.

Losing the war is not the worst thing for us. What is almost unbearable is that we were tricked out of our revolution.

17 June

I visit Annette's grave for the last time. It is pouring.

"The day was storm-tossed and the rain was heavy."

Brahms echoes in me. I say farewell to Meersburg.

Vienurovsky is staying on for a few days. We shake hands. "I'll see you in Munich." He gives me *The Idiot* as a keepsake. He has written something on the flyleaf, in his characteristic vertical hand: "Ivan Vienurovsky, Moscow."

The ship's bell strikes. Meersburg vanishes in the gray rain.

My heart beats faster: I will be in the city again tomorrow. Hertha Holk!

Constance: the old Council Building, the Huss House. I stand at the harbor, yearning for the sea. Around me, a hustle and bustle. On, and on!

18 June

Singing! Hohentwiel! Ekkehard, raw and defiant! Memories of blissful high school years.

Evening is thickening. We pass through dark fir forests. Lights blaze up. The city!

I arrive late at night. As if this were my second home. I pass her house. Her window is open. So she is home. I pause for a moment.

A note lies on my table: "I expect you tomorrow, I am looking forward to it so much. Hertha Holk."

I drop upon the bed, exhausted.
Home!

19 June
Corpus Christi! The procession advances through the streets.
Colors, flags, singing and praying. Children in white, girls in
Black Forest costumes with colorful kerchiefs, earnest, dignified
men, and elderly matrons.
I see her at the cathedral. Bashfulness, embarrassment.
"So you're here!"
"Yes!"
"What a splendid summer day!"
"Yes, and how happy and festive the people all are."
A pause.
How beautiful you are, Hertha Holk!

We ride out that afternoon.
Through dust and summer heat.
And then a long evening full of silence.
Peace! Security!

My heart is filled with intense happiness, and I only wish that
time would stand still.

21 June
"You are an idealist, Michael, even in your attitude towards
women."
"I take things as they are, as they happen to me. Before I let
myself be convinced of evil, I believe in good. But I do not do so
with my intellect. I feel it."
"You are one of the few people who can see the essence
beyond the surface. You think coherently, I might also say
organically. But sometimes you overlook details and things that
are seemingly unimportant, and you then become unfair to
them. This sometimes makes you look unsophisticated. You
often bypass the basics. Life is so strange."

"I think and act as I have to think and act. That is true of anyone who is not part of the herd. We are impelled by a demon who guides us along the prescribed path. We have no choice. That is the way it is."

"You think artistically even in politics. That can sometimes be dangerous for your life and your progress."

"What do you mean progress? I still have two healthy arms to work with."

A pause.

"You also see women differently from what they are. You turn them into what you want them to be. Some day, you will be terribly disappointed. A woman is neither an angel nor a devil. She is a human being and usually not even an important one. And in addition, she has the most lamentable calling. While a man masters life, she masters the cooking pot. Many of the best women today are turning against this. But it doesn't help. In the end, they always come back to the cooking pot. That is the dreadful thing."

"Yet there are courageous women who go beyond that. Besides, giving birth is the highest calling a human being can practice."

"Giving birth? Today? That is almost a contradiction in terms. What thinking mother could accept the responsibility of bringing children into the world if we cannot guarantee them even the most primitive basics?"

"That is a foregone conclusion: Mothers who bear children must have husbands who defend the children's lives, and if life is lost, they must conquer it. . . ."

"One can easily fool oneself. Your idea is correct only if the entire nation thinks in the same way. The individual destroys himself in the struggle against obstacles that the nation as a whole can so easily overcome. But our nation no longer thinks in those terms. We have allowed its spirit of resistance to bleed to death uselessly during the four years of the war."

"Uselessly? Never! It only seems to be that way. The war was the great manifestation of our will to live. And even if we did not attain our goal, our mission lies before us again, as fateful as ever. If our nation no longer thinks in those terms, then we must simply teach it these ideas again."

"Easier said than done. Who can do that?"

"We all can!"

"We? For instance, you?"

"Indeed!"

"I have felt this necessary duty for a long time now, but I have not yet found the redeeming words. I feel as if someone else, a greater man, were maturing already. Some day, he will stand up among us and preach faith in the life of our Fatherland. Many people feel as I do, but only one man can put it into words. Something is evolving. Everyone who is bound with all his strength to the soul of the era senses it. Someone shall come! If I did not have the faith, I would not know how to go on living."

"You say it so casually. That man will sacrifice you, he will sacrifice the ultimate blossoming of our youth."

"Geniuses use up people. That is simply the way things are. However—and this is our solace—geniuses do so not for themselves, but for their mission. One may use up a country's youth if one can thereby free the way to life for a new youth. Besides, it makes no sense to argue about it. These things are inevitable. A youth that is not everlastingly prepared to sacrifice itself silently for the future is simply not a youth.

"That is how youth differs from old age. Old age is an owner, and an owner defends only his property. He sees no need to attack. Only the man deprived of his rights attacks. Indeed, even though it has full power, old age is usually too cowardly even to attack."

"And you want to exclude us women from this struggle?"

"Yes, to an extent, yes! A woman's task is to be beautiful and to bring children into the world. That is not as crude and unmodern as it sounds. The female bird preens herself for her husband and hatches the eggs for him. The husband, in turn, obtains the food. He also stands guard and keeps the enemy at bay.

"What does *reactionary* mean? It is only a catchword. I hate loud women who butt into everything but understand nothing. They usually forget their true mission: To rear children. If modern is synonymous with unnatural, immoral, depraved, and systematic degeneration, then I am deliberately reactionary.

"Being modern is nothing but filling ever new forms with eternal contents. That is what I am doing, after all.

"I emphatically refuse to allow a degenerate hack reporter to teach me what is modern. We young men have gone through too much without—indeed usually against—these line padders. They disgusted and offended us. While an entire nation lies dying, its corrupt intelligentsia proclaims what is modern: films, monocles, bobbed hair, and the *garçone* look. Thanks, anyway."

"At least you're arguing logically."

"I think so too. That is what gives us young men our invincible strength; that is what our oppponents lack: logical thinking. Our philosophy is not made up, it has grown organically, and that is why it stands up even against the harshness and cruelty of life."

"You call that philosophy? That crude, primitive doctrine of existence?"

"Yes, indeed! Philosophy is a point of view: I stand at a solid point and view life and the world from a very specific angle. This has nothing to do with knowledge, much less education. If the point is correct and the angle straight, then the view is clear and good; if not, then it is hazy and bad."

"You always make my heart heavy."

"Without meaning to. But it is good that I do so. We have no reason to take life lightly. It *is* hard after all."

"Yes, it is very hard."

"The best thing people can do is to hold fast to themselves. Everything else is changeable and vanishes in unhappiness like chaff in the wind."

"And the great unknown: God?"

"God helps the bold and strikes down the craven. It would be a strange god who sided with the coward."

"Then let us be bold and look life straight in its relentless face."

"Yes, let us do so."

We both fall silent, and then we talk about trivial things.

Hertha Holk may talk about trivial things, but on her lips they take shape and form. Her words are graphic, palpable.

She is a realist.

25 June

A silent summer afternoon!

Sunshine lies on the deep green mountains. The town below in the valley.

The red rooftops glow.

Wind wafts softly across the peaks, caressing its way across the meadows.

Dark firs in the background.

We sit on the slope and read the book about the twilight distance and the solid, virile present, *Green Henry*.

Proud Judith, gracious Anna.

The chapter is finished. Waiting, silence, quiet!

A thousand insects hum in the grass. It emits a spicy scent.

Everything together produces a hush in nature.

I kiss Hertha Holk on her soft, dreamy mouth; we are both immensely embarrassed.

A thousand insects hum in the grass. It emits a spicy scent.

A silent summer afternoon!

Sunshine lies on the deep green mountains. The town below in the valley.

The red rooftops glow.

Wind wafts slowly across the peaks, caressing its way across the meadows.

Dark firs in the background.

Hertha Holk!

Proud Judith!

Gracious Anna!

The walk home! The setting sun.

My soul is shaken and wrought up.
We part on the street. Her eyes are like two big grayish-green enigmas.

I carry my happiness like a sweet burden.

Night!
I stroll through fields and meadows. I breathe the fragrance of wild roses.
Solitude!
I yearn for something that I cannot put into words.
Yellow moonlight flashes on the roads.
I walk back to town. Roses, pale red roses hang from every garden wall. I pick more and more of them.

I stand at Hertha Holk's window. Dark silence!
Can I hear her breathing? I wait and wait.
Geranium bushes tremble at her window.

I place the bouquet of red roses on her windowsill.
Blissful walk home!

And now a yearning has been realized in me.
Deepest desire becomes deepest pain.
I have stepped into a new world:
One level higher.
There is an urge in me and a longing for new goals and fulfillments.
All strength collects in me for new gifts and virtues.
Night to day!
Blessed hour!

26 June
Hertha Holk wears a red rose on her bosom.

29 June
In me I feel
Word after word growing
Thought after thought lining up

For the last act of Creation,
Holy hour of birth,
You are pain and pleasure
And a yearning
For form, substance, and essence.
I am only an instrument
On which our ancient God
Sings his song.
I am only a waiting vessel,
Which Nature, smiling,
Fills with the new wine.

1 July

Gift-giving is a difficult art. The person who gives shame-facedly understands this art much better than the one who thinks that the recipient ought to be shamefaced.

Hertha Holk gives the way the gods give—she is indiscriminate, unreflecting, with a sheer joy in giving and a wealth of kindness.

She has a divine hand.

She gives and then instantly forgets that she has given.

This diary is my best friend. I can tell it everything. I cannot confide in anyone else in this way. And one does have to tell such things; otherwise, one is never rid of them. They would consume your heart.

The old must go in order to make room for the new. A human soul has too little space to accommodate both. Now and then, one must dump out the old plunder.

This book is something like a garret for me: One stores the things that one no longer needs, that virtually stand in your way.

Sometimes I read an earlier page, sometimes I take an idea, a mood back into my mind, my heart.

Just like browsing through an old garret.

Richard is here!

Old Goethe: He was so precise. And he wrote many things that were very precise. Roundness is boring. No matter how you turn it, it remains round and beautiful.

I love corners, edges, cracks.

I show Richard a picture of Dostoyevsky. How tattered, how furrowed, and demolished!

That is what Michelangelo looks like: the face of a martyr, a prophet.

A man, a fighter, a sufferer, a conquerer, a prophet, an idiot, a hero, and a poet: That is what they all look like.

Goethe has a beautiful head: noble, wonderfully proportioned and chiseled. Like an artwork, like a good thought: a darling of the gods.

Beethoven looks terrible. But his face is as dear to me as my mother's.

Richard does not like the young. He calls their eruptions "sweaty wrestling."

He is right about some things. The young literati say too much, they are not delicate. They misuse language. That is a sin.

The symbol is divine. It is divine because it can only be sensed, never seen.

The noisy bunch of young literati tear the holiest things down into the baseness of the day.

There are things that should not be said. These are usually the deepest and most beautiful. If one does say them, one is being flat and tasteless.

An art without delicacy is swill.

The money that I do not have but that I require for my small daily needs—I am sick of it.

Life is so simple if one only reduces it to its original formula. Most of the things that one calls problems are sheer nonsense. The heart so easily solves all the things that the mind has tormented itself with for centuries.

4 July

Hertha Holk and I are going to the Black Forest.

A dismal, rainy afternoon. We walk along the wide highway. Black woods are shrouded in fog. We wade through mire.

Rain strikes our faces. Soaked through, we arrive in a small guesthouse.

We have supper with the family. It is warm and cozy here. Outside, the water runs down the window panes.

We are the only guests.

In the evening, we sit at the window, watching the rain. Hertha Holk tells me stories.

5 July

The morning begins to clear up, but it is still cool and wet. Onward, across the mountain!

We find a tiny hamlet. Obersteig! We find lodgings.

A beautiful afternoon! Almost autumnal. Nature seems a bit weary.

The landlady is unfriendly and pushy.

In the morning, we go on.

6 July

Breitnau! We have found a clean, simple guesthouse. We wash the dirt from our clothes and hands at the courtyard well; today is Sunday.

By noon, the day is burning hot.

A cow bellows in the byre. The small boy drives out the sheep herd.

July! Sunday afternoon! People rest.

A hot mist rises from the fields. The grain sways in long billows.

The streets are still. We see the village houses through the shimmering gold of the sheaves.

The wind tenderly caresses the stalks.

I seek a sheave that resembles you, Hertha Holk. It is tall and slender and it softly bows its head.

It is so warm here!

We lie in the colorful solitude of the field.

Hush! Silence!

Now and then, we hear the hour striking from the nearby churchtower.

Children sing in the church. A reedy organ accompanies them.
Then silence again.
The bees hum.

Evening! A wind comes, cool.
Red glow on paths and fields.
The ave ringing! A shimmering day wanes.

> When such a summer's day
> Comes to an end,
> The world is bathed in gold,
> The sheaves stand.
> A puff of wind wafts softly
> Through the field of sheaves,
> And the world sinks away
> Like a beautiful dream.

8 July
I have taken along a great dramatic project; everything is completed in my head, only the conclusion is missing.
The problem of our century: starting, but not completing; wanting to, but not being able to.
Something breaks through in me. Love supplies creative energy.
Every man of caliber has some mission to carry out, somewhere, at some time.
I want to write about what I have wrested from my own life in great, difficult hours.

Richard was back home. He brings me greetings from my mother.

In a constant exchange, Hertha Holk gives me joy and strength. I cannot thank her enough.

12 July
I converse with Christ. I believed I had overcome him, but I

have only overcome his idolatrous priests and false servants.

Christ is harsh and relentless.

He drives the Jewish money-changers out of the temple.

A declaration of war against money.

If a man said that today, he would wind up in prison or a madhouse.

We are all sick! Only the fight against corruption can save us again.

Hypocrisy is the characteristic trait of the declining bourgeois era.

The ruling class is weary and has no courage for new things.

Intellect has poisoned our nation.

Hertha Holk looks at me, shaking her head.

15 July

Richard calls me a visionary.

I lie awake night after night, struggling with the powers that attack me.

I am filled with revolt, rebellion, revolution.

An idea inside me grows into grandiose forms.

Dance of death, and resurrection.

16 July

I feel as if I were not living in this world. I race in intoxication, in dreams, in fury.

I sense new worlds.

Remoteness grows in me.

Help me, oh God, to say what I suffer!

I read Nietzsche's sermons, *The Gay Science*.

19 July

Christ is the genius of love.

He is the greatest and most tragic man who ever lived on earth.

Hertha Holk believes in me as she believes in the gospel.

21 July

Silent days are coming. I yearn for fulfillment.

We must come to terms, Hertha Holk and I.

23 July

Life is awful in these days.

Convulsion, burning restlessness, strife with God and the devil, war for spiritual existence.

Why do I find no fulfillment?

I wish to be calm and wait for redemption.

I feel something like the future in me.

One always finds greatness in creative solitude. My hour, too, shall strike.

The mind has begun to march.

I believe again.

25 July

Illumination has come upon me.

I am writing a play. Its hero is Jesus Christ.

I am silent and blissfully receptive. Everything is new for me and unknown.

Now, a flower, a poem, a picture becomes an experience for me.

I thank the Lord!

27 July

Richard has left. He has gone home!

Greetings to my mother and the village, the vast, silent fields, and that path, you know, behind the church, where the pussy willows bloom.

The semester is over. I spend my last evening with Hertha Holk.

Farewell! *Auf Wiedersehen.*

I shall then be a different man.

She goes to the red land.
"I am taking along your strength and kindness. Farewell!"

30 July
This is my last day in the town. Alone. It disgusts me.
Boxes and suitcases helter-skelter in my room.
Hertha Holk's last message on an open slip of paper:
"You shall grow from my waning strength. It is a great joy to make sacrifices for the things one loves."

I am going to the sea. The roaring of the ocean! Solitude! Infinity! One's thoughts become as vast and clear as the sea.

31 July
The train rolls out of the town. There is the castle mountain.
Tears come to my eyes.
On! On!

1 August
Through the coal-mining area. Hertha Holk's homeland. Rain smacks against the panes.
Gray fog! Smoke! Noise! Screeching! Groaning! Flames flaring up against the sky!
Symphony of labor!
A grand work of the human hand!

My brothers in the mines and workshops, I greet you!

Plain! Meadows of rich grass! Cattle grazing.
The day clears up. Sunshine breaks through. The windows down.
One can almost smell salt.
I stand at the window. My heart is bursting. I am sheer expectation.
North! "Five more minutes," a woman says, smiling.
There it rises, in the distance. Blue—gray.
Infinity! That is the sea!
Thalatta! I would like to shout.

That was how the Greeks greeted the ocean.
Thalatta! Thalatta!

Into the boat. Waves splash over my face and hands. How delightful!
A rocking ride. Land vanishes in the evening. The round sun sinks into endlessness.
In the distance, a dot. Land! The sailor signals with his shoulder:
The island.
Safe! Alone!
In a large ship, and sea all around.
The island!
The blessed land.

"I am certainly a flame!"

2 August
Last night, the storm sang its wild songs on the panes.
Now, the world is silent.
Day is dawning. A pale red cloud drifts across the tideland.
After a while, the sun rises.
I walk along untrodden paths, through the white dunes, towards the sea.
This morning rises, so dewy-fresh!
In the distance, the waves beat upon the beach. One can hear their monotonous roar.
Up on the dune, one can see far across the ocean.
Lurking, insidious, tremendous! It lies there!
I look down, my eye scouring the endless surface.
White lights float very far away. That is where the high seas begin.
One sees the waves beating down. They come nearer and nearer and then sweep, softly swaying, across the strand.
The surface of the water shines, almost blue-violet. The air smells of grass and seaweed.
I go down to the beach. The tide is starting to come in. This is the first time I have ever watched it.
An eternal circulation.

The jetties are deserted. I stand in water and have to keep going back as the tide moves in.

An ebb and flow, back and forth.

Then a wave springs up. Foam sprays into my face, my tongue tastes salt.

I stand, gazing, until the tide is in.

The waves wash over the fortifications, roaring, abrupt, as in a raging fury.

Foam sprays white.

The water retreats, then slams forward with incredible strength.

Infinite nature!

How small we are. Tiny humans!

Children playing on the beach, building houses and castles.

A tall Friesian boatsman walks along the narrow path, earnest and reflective.

4 August

Ebb tide.

I sit on a plank on the beach, writing the great scene in which Jesus sits among the Jewish sages in the temple.

7 August

A letter from Hertha Holk:

> I am sending you this picture of the Seven Swans. It will bring you joy. I feel as if it ought to remind you, too, of wonderful days.
>
> I know you are living in a dichotomy. Never forget, do you hear, that my love for you keeps my eyes open to everything concerning you.
>
> How discouraged I feel because you are so far away. Sometimes I doubt your love, and then I would like to cry my eyes out. Forgive me! Sometimes I lie awake until late at night and long for your solid pride.
>
> I know you will find your path, for you are strong and you have faith in the future.
>
> But you should take life as it is. We can change very lit-

tle. You will save yourself some meandering. But I know that you will reply: The meanderings are the best part of a journey. Still, the straight and narrow path never leads one astray.

Your Hertha Holk

The Seven Swans hangs next to my bed.

9 August

They call this place a hotel. Back home, we would be more modest and call it a guesthouse.

The guests are pleasant. Teachers, pastors, government workers. Many children. I like that very much. Day by day, one sees them getting fresher and healthier.

And the nicest thing about this island is that people do not bother you. You can do whatever you like.

There is an atmosphere of mutual good will.

One can work in peace and quiet.

The spa of the educated, little people, the landlord says, laughing.

I share a table with a musician. We talk about Wagner, the musical drama, and we never reach a conclusion.

Music is music. This is evidently known as absolute music.

Mozart did not need a program for his music. He played and sang with the divine ease of a child.

I would like to be a pastor on this island. Explain the Sermon on the Mount to simple people and let the world be the world.

I have not seen any Jews as of yet. That is a true delight.

I am physically disgusted by Jews. I feel nauseated at the mere sight of one.

The Jew, in his essence, is the very opposite of us. I cannot hate him, I can only scorn him. He has raped our people, sullied our ideals, and paralyzed the strength of our nation, corrupting our morals and spoiling our ethics.

He is the ulcer on the body of our sick populace.

Religion? How naive you are. What does that have to do with religion, much less Christianity? Either he will destroy us or we must render him harmless. No other choice is conceivable.

Peace? Can a lung infected by the tuberculosis bacillus keep peace?

The Jew is not creative. He is a tradesman by nature. He trades in everything: rags, money, stocks, cures, paintings, books, political parties, and nations.

Should we become as smart as he? He is not the least bit smart. He is merely sly, wily, crafty, cunning, and unscrupulous. We shall not imitate him.

The people wants, says the Jew. In reality, he is the one who wants. He hides behind the nation, wearing a mask of friendliness towards the masses in order to pursue his goals all the more ruthlessly. The nation wants nothing. It only wants to be governed decently.

The Jew screams until the German gives in to him just to make him stop screaming.

He who cannot hate the devil cannot love God. He who loves his nation must hate the destroyer of his nation, hate him from the depths of his soul.

Being praised by a Jew is the worst punishment that a German can endure.

When the Jew wants a little finger, he screams at the top of his lungs: I have to have the whole hand. And the German then goes halfway and gives him two fingers.

Christ cannot have been a Jew. I do not need to prove this with science or scholarship. It is so!

12 August

A stroll through the tidal fields. Sheep and cattle graze. The sea across the mud flats lies calm, like a mirror.

A light sailboat moves across the water. It almost hovers between the sky and the sea.

The coast appears far in the distance. Roofs and towers blur in the gray mist.

Behind me and before me, the red roofs of the houses on the island. One can see far, far away. The horizon is refreshingly pure.

My legs are tired. I am so cozy and contented.

I would like to do something. Write an essay that will create a stir, anything to get rid of this excess energy.

Work sets me free. I cannot get away from it.

I sit on the beach every day, composing my whispering verses. The sea provides the rhythms.

My pen has wings. Three scenes have been put to paper.

Pouring your heart's blood into a mold is the deepest happiness. I write the torment and disquiet out of my soul.

The joy of creation!

In the evening, I sit in my room and read the Bible. The sea roars in the distance.

Then I lie awake for a long time, thinking about the pale, silent man from Nazareth.

14 August

Dear Hertha Holk,

This is my dichotomy, which you have recognized. I tell you what I can tell you now. I live here, silent and lonesome, nourishing my soul with the comfort of work. You understand what I mean.

You always understand me.

Let us be still
And wait,
Until a star falls from the sky.
Do you see up there, light
Kindling light
To form a cathedral!
We sit in silence,
Folding our hands
In prayer.
Let us be still
And wait
Until a star falls from the sky.

The Seven Swans gives me great joy.

I am seeking a path.

Have faith and you shall find.

17 August

A small, bare room. Tall Friesian women in their local costumes sit on the chairs. Organ music. The schoolmaster plays. A chorale rises.

The plain words of a young pastor.

Sunday morning sunlight flashes on the meadows outside.

The island is not large. One can walk across it in two hours. A dozen houses in the Western village, even fewer in the Eastern village.

In between lie the dunes and tidal flats.

The houses are clean and the roofs are red. This gives the entire island a friendly look.

The Eastern village, which lies hidden behind foliage, is inhabited by retired sailors and fishermen.

On Sunday mornings, the tourists stroll back and forth between the two villages.

The mood between the hours of eleven and one is almost festive. One sees nothing but friendly faces. Children play with the sheep on the tidal flats.

People wander around the island until noon.

I pray to my destiny, begging it to prevent me from becoming mediocre, to make me nothing or everything.

Doing one's duty means doing what one has recognized on one's own as being right.

We do not need men, we need one man.

My path: from the individual to the totality, from the phenomenon to the symbol, from the brother to the nation, and only from the nation to the world.

The smaller the man, the less able he is to believe.

20 August
> I always want to fly and yet I crawl in the filth.
> Till we meet again! When and where?
>
> Richard

Christ on Mount Olympus. A grandiose idea.

Zeus and Christ as adversaries. What a subject!

Christ measures men by his standards. That is why he perishes in the end. Incidentally, that is the tragedy of nearly all prophets and great revolutionaries. They see others as they themselves are. That is the error in their calculation.

If Christ came back, how quickly he would take a whip and

drive his false servants out of his temple!

When I sit by the sea in the morning, composing verses and inhaling the salty wind, which wafts over from the water, I am absorbed in God and I am as happy as I was in my childhood.

24 August

A narrow trail runs straight through the dunes. I slowly follow it, taking along the monotonous roar of the sea until it becomes softer. Increasingly softer.

The path runs up and down the dunes.

It is very difficult walking through thistles and hard, woody reeds.

I descend into a final dune valley. And now the sea is silent. I hear nothing.

A wondrous hush emerges.

I lie down in the dunes and wait for a word from God's lips.

28 August

My mother works from early morning until late at night, and she is happy doing so. If everyone else is content, then she, too, is content.

My mother makes constant sacrifices for her children.

She never feels lonely. I learned this ability from her.

I have never seen my mother idle.

> I am happy, dear mother, that I can find myself in this solitude. I often think of home. I see father walking through the field and the farm. You are going through a hard time since the harvest is just around the corner. Sometimes I do not feel right about being so idle. But I know you understand me: We young men who went through the war have to deal with ourselves in so many ways. Our souls are still in pain. A shattered arm is not the worst thing; far worse are internal wounds inflicted by war and destruction. We are no longer free and calm in regard to God and the world.
>
> And yet, some day we shall be resurrected. Our eyes shall see straight and clear again. Just let us be. Seek and ye shall find.

29 August

The inhabitants of the island are upright and proud, the women strong and healthy. The eternal surge of the waves is inscribed in the eyes of these people.

The sea is their universe. Their pride, their solace, their God. Here, on this island, they are strong men. Supermen! In our cities, they would be poor, lost children.

That is why the people of these islands never yearn for the sinful mainland.

This afternoon, I lie in a dune. A child passes me, weeping. She has gotten lost in the dunes. I carry her back to her mother.

She is Friesian, still young. Tall, slender, tanned by the hard sun of the dunes. She pours a glass of milk for me. I sit down at the table, and she tells me about her husband and children.

Her husband is shopping on the mainland.

The little girl already trusts me, she chatters near me and plays by my knees. I give her chocolate and a picture by Schwind, which I happen to have in my pocket.

She doesn't seem to care much about the picture, but she eats the chocolate with great delight.

The young, beautiful mother blushes and seems embarrassed when I take my leave.

Children are as cruel and heartless as nature.

A child laughs when it feels joy and weeps when it feels pain. It puts its whole heart into both—laughter and weeping.

We have all become so big and smart. We know so much and have read so much. But there is one thing we have forgotten: How to laugh and weep like a child.

31 August

It is such a pleasure to feel everything working in us. I live here as if I were in a different world.

At work, I am cheerful and in high spirits.

I struggle hard with the forms, through which the contents seem ready to burst. The great subject matter rips apart the narrow confines of moderation. I cannot tame the verses. They tumble over the lines.

The first act is completed. I believe it is successful.
I barely come to my senses.

2 September
"I trust you. I shall wait until a star falls from the sky."

3 September
Afternoon. Ebb tide!
I stand on a wharf.
Now, the world is silent. The sea, which was raging so mightily this morning, is as friendly as a beloved. People are walking in the distance. The landscape is so silent that one can hear them laughing and shouting.

A fisherman stands on the other wharf. A sharp stroke against the clear horizon.

One sees nothing but white dune sand. Everything rising from the earth looks large, sharp, like a silhouette.

If one gazes for a long time, the people down below suddenly grow into different dimensions. Everything becomes immense, and then one sees only black and white.

Eventually, the colors vanish entirely; only strokes and lines remain visible.

I walk down along the beach, far across the island, thinking of Hertha Holk.

A woman without grace is like a house without an entrance. Both remain closed.

Hertha Holk is very middle-class. She does not have the courage to get out of herself, to be herself.

She is like a child: unreflecting, naive, pure in both joy and pain. She lavishes gifts of kindness and mildness.

She loves like a queen.

The true woman loves the eagle.

The lesser woman clips its wings and makes it a pet.

That is what we are witnessing today: A class has carried out its historical mission and is about to make way for the creative will of a new, young class. The bourgeoisie is yielding to the proletariat. This has nothing to do with callings. The ultimate decision lies in one's spiritual stance. One does not become middle-class. One *is* middle-class!

One class overcomes the preceding one only in powerful, revolutionary upheavals.

Bourgeois—what a terrible insult.

If something is falling, we have to push it.

We are all soldiers in the revolution of labor. We want the victory of labor over money. That is socialism. At the moment, socialism is following various directions, but the will is the same everywhere. This is our ultimate comfort; we need not despair.

In its decline, the gradually crumbling historical class is once again putting forth the finest blossoms of its moribund creative energy. The ignorant readily tend to see this as newly awakened productivity. But that is not so. Once again, nourished by nearly buried channels, excellence and grace gather together in the last days of a dying world, and, in its death, shape creatures of pure beauty and grace.

Perhaps that is Hertha Holk's secret. Who knows?

I have overcome. I have cleared away any vestiges of the past within me; I have cleared them away ruthlessly and relentlessly.

I am a revolutionary. I say this with proud awareness. I have never been anything else; nor can I ever be anything else.

8 September

In the evening, the tourists stand on the landing stage. The passenger boat is coming. People wave back and forth. Like a big family.

Welcome to our island!

The sailors yell, the boat is moored, the engine is still rattling.

In the distance, a boat is rocking on the waves. People peer through binoculars.

Yes indeed, the mail boat!

We keep waiting. It arrives within half an hour. The tourists themelves drag the mail sacks to the nearby post office.

There will be mail tonight.

Thank goodness!

People sit at the inn, waiting. Here comes the mail! Everyone pounces on it.

A letter from Munich. From Ivan Vienurovsky.
    Come to Munich this winter. This is the German city in
which one can learn a lot. Berlin is awful. It's the German
St. Petersburg. Munich has a different air. You will meet
many new people here. Russians! Whether or not you
believe it, Russians are human beings too.

Every age has its great idea. And every idea is correct in its
time.
The idea that has the strongest advocates is the one that wins
out.

9 September
The children play in the sand. I like watching them. Children
are imaginative.
    One boy is building an entire house: living room, bedroom,
parlor, kitchen. He explains the construction to me, proud and
joyful. When I walk by, he stretches out wide on a bed in his
sand-dune bedroom so that I notice him. I walk over and show
my great interest.
    He gets lost in details.
    I ask him a lot of questions. He answers modestly; he is well
brought up. His name is Gustav Adolf, and he comes from
Hamburg.
    He asks me what my name is, my profession: a student?
    "I want to be a student too. But I'd like to study in
Heidelberg. I want to be an engineer."
    "Then you can't study in Heidelberg."
    "No? Why not?"
    I explain why; he is very disappointed.
    He looks around for his little friends. "Those kids are up to no
good," he says precociously.
    He wants to visit me on the wharf later on. "Where you
always sit."
    We instantly become good friends.

    I lean back in the deck-chair on the wharf, very close to the water, and let the tiny waves play around me.

Individual verses go through my mind. I am too lazy to write.

Sweet idleness!

I sit and sit, not thinking.

I merely watch the waves.

The way they come and go in everlasting alternation.

This is profoundly restful.

Gustav Adolf looks for me on the wharf. He instantly calls me Michael.

He has built a castle for me on the beach.

"You can sit in it only when the sun shines," he says. "This house is only for high tide because the wind is very sharp."

I thank him profusely.

I sit with him in my newly built castle. Then he starts talking about Hamburg. Everything, even the smallest details, the way children talk.

I enjoy listening to him.

"You're really brown as a nut," he says suddenly.

"Yes!"

I want to add something, but he starts talking again.

"Tomorrow I can lend you my spade. The wind will blow sand into the castles at night."

"Are you enjoying yourself here?" I ask.

"Yes, but I'd rather be in Hamburg."

He is accompanied by a governess.

In the evening, I sit with Gustav Adolf and his friends. I show photographs to the boys and then play ditties on the piano for them.

11 September

Gustav Adolf has used seashells to write "Villa Michael" on my castle.

He is my best friend.

13 September

The air is cool. The wind is icy. One can no longer lie on the beach.

Many guests have left. The guesthouse is emptying out.

I have completed half the second act. But I seem to have a block.

I can't get any further. I feel wiped out.

I often sit with Gustav Adolf for hours. I tell him about the universities. He is very interested.

The faculty of amazement: That is the source of all poetry and philosophy.

Nature is the mother of us all.

A strong book gives us strength. But only if we are strong ourselves.

Drama is action intensified into passion.

If you want to depict action, you must know how to act.

Devotion, ardor, yearning! Those are my pillars.

We have to be a bridge to the future.

When I redeem myself, I redeem my people.

17 September

Gustav Adolf has left with his friends.

"I'll write you from Hamburg," he says at his departure. "And you can use my house, of course."

He is referring to the sand castle he so arduously built out on the beach.

He waves to me from the boat for a long time. I watch the little boat through my binoculars until it vanishes completely.

I can still see Gustav Adolf standing at the sail with his friends, acting like an expert.

And now I feel lonely and forlorn here.

20 September

My work is flowing again.

I write with love and energy.

I sit in my room. The beach is already icy cold.

21 September

I've got the feel of it again, the tone. My pen is flying over the pages.

Create! Create!

25 September
Overnight the sea has swept into the mud flats.
Spring tide!
We are cut off from the world. No mail can come in or go out.
The Last Judgment is thundering on the beach. I holler at the storm, it takes my breath away.
One is carried, one flies.
The waves rage! The distant whitecaps surge.
The sea howls, hollers, shrieks, hisses, whistles.
The sea, the vast sea! The giant monster!
We human beings should keep still.
Upheaval! Adoration!

28 September
We are cut off from the world. No mail, no letters, no newspapers.
Wonderful security! We are alone in the world.
Alone in the world for the first time.
I write breathlessly as if I had to die tomorrow.

The sea is a great devil.

30 September
It is silent now. The sea has raged itself out.
Now it lies like a vast, flat land, gray, blue.
The last storms are gone. Outside and inside.
I am purged.
Completely free.
The first two acts are on paper.
That is all I can say now.
I have nothing more to say.

1 October
The mail arrives. A letter from Hertha Holk, she is in Munich.

> I have been in Munich for a week now and expect you soon. Everything is ready for your arrival. I have rented a

lovely room for you out in Schwabing.

Munich is the right place for you. Art, intellect, and a people attached to the soul. You will be absolutely delighted.

You seem like a new man in your letters. You are a different person. I am really looking forward to your arrival! I miss you terribly. I am nothing without you.

The bags are packed. Now off into the world. The walls are collapsing upon me.

My wings are beating!

The next stage is beginning.

I run down the beach again. The sun sets, blood red.

Upstairs, on my suitcase lies a pack of white paper. The first page says *Jesus Christ, a Dramatic Fantasy*. The second page says "Dedicated to Hertha Holk."

Munich!

The next stage!

4 October

Riding through night!

In the distance, a sea of lights flashes up: Munich!

I take a deep breath.

Munich air!

I am overcome by the whimsical frivolity of an artist.

Hertha Holk is standing on the platform. Altered, somewhat strange, I barely recognize her. She looks and looks. All at once, she spies me, dashes towards me.

Michael!

Our hellos go on and on.

Welcome to Munich.

7 October

We wander along Kaufingerstrasse. It is six p.m.

A life!

Tyroleans in mountain costumes, artists in trilby hats, soldiers, girls, women, neatly dressed gentlemen; cars zooming by, coaches creeping arduously through the commotion.

Here, an excited conversation; there, a cluster of people.

People barely notice. We breathe the soft air of Munich, the city of artists.

In the huge beer-gardens, the Munich philistines sit over their beers. The air smells warmly of supper-time.

Outdoors, it is already cold. Autumn in Munich is delightful. A big city, but not a metropolis.

A human being is as he laughs.

12 October

"Sometimes I can hardly understand you anymore."

"That is because things are only just starting in me. We have no time to remain the same for long. We must forge ahead into infinity. Deeper and deeper, more and more earnest, more and more silent.

"We cannot articulate everything that takes place within us. We scarcely know it ourselves. Sometimes I stand still and listen. We can do little about the things that dissolve and then cohere again within us."

"You treat yourself as if you were a second person. You observe yourself. You separate yourself from yourself. You analyze yourself. You are no longer what you used to be. You will be lonely."

"We are always twofold."

"Yes, but that's not the right thing for you. You are interested in yourself, you are becoming an eccentric."

"A human soul is only the small image of the world. We have already spoken about those antitheses: macrocosm and microcosm.

"What confuses me outside, frightens, makes me indignant is something I see becoming clearer and more uniform in me."

"The modern spirit can never bypass aestheticism."

"Ah, with aestheticism so much is shrugged off today, things the coarse bourgeois mind does not understand.

"Is it wrong of us to be more serious, more taciturn, more

thoughtful, more complicated? Is this not what our time is like?"

"But the human element is lighter, more carefree, simple."

"I don't know, I am so deeply tormented by these questions, but I cannot force myself. I must clear the way myself. One must promote what is inside oneself and then wait."

"That is the beginning of the ethics of the weak: Living one's life—that is the simplest thing in the world."

"Yes, living in the mind, the mind is free.

"The body is bound. Absolute living is merely slavish drudgery."

"One cannot take the first step so lightly. The path descends steeply and quickly."

"You no longer believe in me."

"If I no longer believe in you, then what should I believe in?"

The fog thickens gray from the vast flatland of the English Garden.

Only dark shadows of trees are visible.

It is silent here.

The noise of the city is far away.

14 October

These are the final lovely autumn days.

The red-brown gold shimmers on the trees.

A walk along the Isar River.

Far away, you can see the clear outlines of towers and the city. The sky is gray and yet refreshingly bright and clear.

The view is delightfully vast. The eyes relax in the lines.

And then the colors, the thousand colors!

Autumn is a fine painter.

Maturation!

We must mature and become the new type.

16 October

At the Pinakothek, I see Dürer's painting of the apostles and am deeply shaken.

18 October

This Schwabing! Munich's Latin Quarter! A neighborhood of eternally seething ferment.

How many artists' dreams and yearnings ascend to the sky here every day.

Artists and misunderstood geniuses, aesthetes and snobs, critics and criticasters, philosophers and would-be philosophers, scholars and pompous fools, God-seekers and God-enjoyers, mystics and ecstatics: the big and the little, showing their stuff—and their nonsense.

This place is marked: by God or the devil. It has an atmosphere of its own.

"The canker known as Munich," a reporter wrote recently.

One feels as if one were sitting on a fire-spewing volcano that is calm for a moment, but seething and rumbling in slow, barely audible waves.

Painters, students, poets, and Schwabing girls move imperiously through the streets. They are at home here.

One hears words that one cannot pronounce. Most of them end with "ism."

Almost everything is coffeehouse literature.

This Schwabing must be fumigated. It is the breeding ground of disintegrating tendencies; and it has nothing to do with the real Munich.

21 October

Hertha Holk and I visit Ivan Vienurovsky. It is evening, and we find him brewing his tea.

Ivan Vienurovsky has become old. He looks weary and tormented. At first he does not recognize me—or is he only pretending? Then he greets us, grouchy and grumpy.

He talks about his revolutionary activity. He worked for the Party, but made himself unpopular, so he was thrown out.

"Those scoundrels are driven by the devil. They are only out for money. The entire revolution is being ruined by human beings. The human rabble is too petty for a new world."

"There are too few people who are ready to make sacrifices. We have to wait. Time is on our side. We have to let time work."

He looks at me, half incredulous, half sarcastic.

"No, that's not it at all. The leaders are failing us. They don't even want a revolution. They laugh if we talk about anything but economy. They lack any sense of grandeur, elan, fire. They are nothing but a bunch of good-for-nothings."

"We have to start with the people. When I regard these matters from the German standpoint, then I see that our terrible problem resides in our being rooted too deeply in false traditions. We are not yet Germans. We have been Germans only now and then, in the very great moments of our history. And yet you come and talk to us about a world republic. That is not suitable for us."

"The idea of a United States of Europe is the smartest idea that anyone has thought up in decades. But it is not the be-all and end-all. It is only a stage. We Russian revolutionaries have set a goal for ourselves: A free man on the free earth."

"That is lovely rhetoric. But it shatters against hard reality. We Germans have enough trouble dealing with ourselves."

"Others will force you. A world idea cannot be smashed by the eccentric reclusiveness of hidebound philistines."

"Really! Forcing takes two. One person to do the forcing and another to be forced."

"For the time being, we are still masters in our own home," Hertha Holk says mockingly.

Ivan Vienurovsky smiles.

He looks worn out.

He now talks to Hertha Holk. Softly, almost in a feminine way. He does not look at her. His eyes are lowered, heavy.

Suddenly he stands up, his face chalky. All at once, that old demonic quality burns in his eyes, a quality that haunts me.

"Yet the day will come sooner or later, it has to come! I shall not live to see it, nor shall you. But it *is* coming! We have not suffered in vain.

"The world cannot forget that Europe's youth bled its last on the battlefields for an idea—unconsciously perhaps—but each soldier felt this idea: The knowledgeable felt it as faith and the faithful as an inkling. One cannot bury youth in silence.

"It makes no difference that we shall not live to see the day. It is fulfillment enough to be the pacemaker and pioneer of a new era. Do not think that we are tilting against windmills. Those in power know what the stakes are. They have merely changed their tactics.

"First, they tried to kill us. Now they merely try to bury us in silence.

"But we shall make ourselves heard.

"Europe has to hear us.

"We are the leaven that makes the world ferment. We are the salt of the earth."

He pauses, exhausted, and gazes at us in utter amazement as if noticing our presence for the first time. Then he lapses into a long silence.

It is late. We leave.

"I hate Ivan Vienurovsky," says Hertha Holk on the way home.

23 October
Expressionism is being destroyed by its own false prophets.

They run after the big men in order to hide behind their coattails and sneak into Mount Olympus.

The fear of the philistine: To be unmodern. That whole rabble consists of literary caricatures.

"I am disgusted by this pen-pushing century!"

The intellectual achievement of our age is the editorial, the Party speech, the parliamentary claptrap.

Books have become a luxury.

Literature has become a matter for political parties.

Goethe's work method: He has an experience, it touches a chord in his breast, the chord quivers in his subconscious for days, for years, eventually it sounds louder, the experience concentrates, it becomes clearer, purer, new experience values are added; and the poet now writes down what is prescribed in his soul.

Goethe is an essential impressionist.

Impression is an imprint, expression is an out-pressing.

Impressionism is the art of impressions, expressionism is the art of expressions. That is the whole secret.

Our decade is entirely expressionist in its internal structure. This has nothing to do with the faddish term.

We people of today are all expressionists. People who want to shape the outside world from within ourselves.

The expressionist is building a new world within him. His secret and his power reside in his ardor. His ideology usually shatters when it collides with reality.

The soul of the impressionist: a microcosmic picture of the macrocosm.

The soul of the expressionist: a new macrocosm. A world of its own.

Expressionist sense of the world is explosive. It is an autocratic sense of being oneself.

24 October

After an evening of pain and happiness, a promise to Hertha Holk:

> I knelt before you
> And asked
> For your soul.
> You gave it to me.
> I enclose it
> In my two hands,
> And I wish to treasure it
> So it will not break;
> It is so fine and delicate,
> Like a south wind
> That sings softly
> On a summer afternoon,
> Against your hot forehead.

27 October

The much-lauded objective science at German universities: "The minds of the masters, in which the times are reflected." Why do they not have the courage to practice free subjectivism?

It is better to be one's own slave than the slave of the object.

I stand in our time on both feet. Stand in its valleys and let its enthusiasms carry me to the stars.
For our contemporaries, there seems to be only one absolute: relativity.

I spend a lot of time in cafes. Here, I meet people from all over the world. One then loves anything German all the more. Unfortunately, that has become so rare in our Fatherland.
Munich is inconceivable without its snobbish Jews.

29 October
Hertha Holk is twenty-three today.
I give her some of my notes and a deluxe edition of *Faust*.
She is delighted.

1 November
Starnberg. The snowy mountains loom in the distance. Breathtakingly beautiful!

A great moment! With the other person, joyful and dreamy together.
Days, years gather.
We are a calm, quiet island in the ocean of the world.
End and beginning!
Border between life and eternity!
Intoxication, intensity, existence! I take my heart in both hands.
I live!
Oh, this wealth of powerful life!
Symbol becomes reality.
Pleasure is torture.
I reel through eternities.
I fall into abysses, deep and immense.
I no longer exist myself!

Thus I must get to know the other person in you.

We travel for a long time in a dark train compartment.
Hertha Holk weeps softly.

4 November
I listened to Beethoven's Ninth Symphony, and at the end I thought that the world would have to collapse.
Everyone fights and struggles as I fight and struggle.
Eternal enigma: birth and death.
Why must we suffer like this?

6 November
   I have deep conflicts with the teachers here. A tiny university aristocracy is unendurable in the long run. One loses one's connection to life. The courses are all right so far—but there's always some element of kitsch. I want to spare you shoptalk, however. Goodness, one certainly gets used to shoptalk here. Our scholarship suffers from the disease of superlatives. Farewell.

                                                              Richard

10 November
Ivan Vienurovsky takes me to an artist's studio. It belongs to a painter from Hamburg and a sculptress from Zurich.
The sculptress is a gentle, lovely girl with blond hair.
The painter is painting a crucifix, lavish in its colors, well thought out; but, like almost all modern painting, it is somewhat overdone.
They fight and argue. Ivan Vienurovsky makes fun of him.
I sit next to the sculptress on a couch. We take little part in the conversation.
Her name is Agnes Stahl, and she is better than my first impression of her.

11 November
The Munich burgher is a philistine. But he has an advantage over the cosmopolitan philistine: He generally leaves the artists alone.

Hertha Holk thinks I ought to start preparing for my degree examinations.

15 November

Hertha Holk and I visit an exhibition of modern painting: We run into Agnes Stahl, the sculptress from Zurich.

We see a lot of new nonsense.

One star: Vincent van Gogh.

In this environment, he seems almost tame, yet he is the most modern among the moderns.

Modernity has nothing to do with heroic gestures. Those things are all learned.

Modernity is a new sense of the world.

The modern man is intrinsically a seeker of God, perhaps a Christ-man.

Van Gogh's life says more to us than his work. He unites the most important things: He is a teacher, a preacher, a fanatic, a prophet—crazy.

After all, we are all crazy if we have an idea.

Fanatic of love: the will to sacrifice!

Life is sacrifice for your neighbor:

And my neighbor is the one with the same blood.

Blood is still the best and the most enduring glue.

How dreadfully difficult is the torment of looking.

The modern German is marked not so much by intelligence and intellect as the new principle, unreflected devotion, sacrifice, loyalty to one's nation.

What a grand image: Van Gogh sitting among the black miners in Belgium, explaining the Sermon on the Mount.

Now I have the term: We modern Germans are something like Christ Socialists.

Christ is the genius of love, as such the most diametrical opposite of Judaism, which is the incarnation of hate. The Jew is a non-race among the races of the earth. His mission in the human organism is the same as that of the poisonous bacillus: To mobilize the resistance of the healthy powers or else force a doomed creature to die more quickly and more soundlessly.

Christ is the first great enemy of the Jews. "You should devour all nations!" He declared war against that. That is why Judaism had to get rid of him. For he was shaking the very foundations of its future international power.

The Jew is the lie personified. When he crucified Christ, he crucified everlasting truth for the first time in history. This was repeated dozens of times during the next twenty centuries and is being repeated again today.

The idea of sacrifice first gained visible shape in Christ. Sacrifice is intrinsic to socialism. Sacrifice oneself for others. The Jew, however, does not understand this at all. His socialism consists of sacrificing others for himself.

This is what Marxism is like in practice.

Distribute your property to the poor: Christ.

Property is theft—so long as it does not belong to me: Marx.

Christ Socialists. That means voluntarily and willingly doing what the run-of-the-mill socialists do out of pity or for reasons of state.

Moral necessity versus political insight.

The struggle we are now waging today until victory or the bitter end is, in its deepest sense, a struggle between Christ and Marx.

Christ: the principle of love.

Marx: the principle of hate.

We sit together in a cafe for a long time. We are still shaken by the exhibition of modern painting. So much aspiration in an era and yet so little talent.

I am so sated by ecstasies of alien fervor that I long for reality.

Is our insatiable yearning to ascend incompatible with the fact that we stand with solid, vigorous bones on the solid, abiding earth?

The alien rabble must leave German art.

The fate of German art is our own good German concern.

The German spirit is still very promising.

When shall those who are quiet in the land begin to speak?

In the time of waiting, we are the nation working towards the future of the Fatherland.

17 November

Hertha Holk is my torment and my redemption. She lets me see heaven and hell.

I can scarcely get along without her in my days of suffering.

23 November

I spend a great deal of time with Ivan Vienurovsky and his Russian friends.

Hertha Holk suffers a great deal because of me.

25 November

Politics corrupts the character.

This is the cheapest excuse of the beer-hall politicians who are not ashamed to boast that they have no opinions of their own.

28 November

A card from Hamburg:

Dear Herr Michael,

Do you still think about the days on our island? I haven't forgotten them. Are you still as tan as you were? I look forward to going to the university.

Best greetings from your loyal friend,

Gustav Adolf

1 December

Schack Gallery. The German poets of painting!

Schwind, Spitzweg. I stood in front of Feuerbach's *Pietà* for a long time.

If you wander aimlessly through Munich, you might suddenly find yourself standing in front of an old house, a secret, dreamlike church, which smiles like a friendly anachronism to our modern haste.

3 December

I saw Hebbel's *Die Nibelungen* in a theater, with red lights and a warm-blue background, measured gestures and restrained ardor in style and language.

Theater becomes an experience.

How easily man with his gifts can come close to perfection.

6 December

Studio party. The large, bare room transformed into a fairy

palace; with a few simple devices, but with style and taste.

The women bathe in colors.

What a mood! One is torn along, tears others along, forgetting and forgiving.

How beautiful life is!

Music and dance!

The violins sigh.

The first champagne cork pops.

And now a wild singing and yelling.

You join in the singing and yelling.

Embraces, friendship, eternal friendship!

What beautiful women! In black and red!

But you are the most beautiful, Hertha Holk!

Agnes Stahl is a Swiss burgher's daughter. We sit together for a long time, and she tells me about her art.

Agnes Stahl and Hertha Holk get along wonderfully.

Agnes Stahl does not talk much, but one likes her silence.

Hey, you party-poopers, go to the devil!

Music and dancing. The violins sob.

Women in black and red.

But you are the most beautiful, Hertha Holk!

7 December

These artists don't take life all too seriously.

Tasteful enjoyment. One has to overcome misery.

The most profound soon separate and go their own way.

But these artists don't take life all too seriously until the end of their days.

9 December

The newspapers bellyache and agitate. Those irresponsible hacks!

The people are out in the streets, rioting and demonstrating. The lords and masters are at the conference table, calmly finishing their game.

The old Europe is going to pot.

Yes, the world is crazy! Economy, Horatio!

One is drawn out into the streets as if by a mysterious power. Your mind is outside, where a piece of history is in the making—no sublime piece, but nevertheless a piece. The serious observer has a lot to think about.

I have reached the point of regarding all this merely as material that helps to shape my inner self.

One must become the focal point around which everything turns.

13 December

I come out of the theater, and Marienplatz is covered with snow. Yellow moonlight plays upon it.

A delightfully dreamy tableau, as in the days of his royal highness.

18 December

Schubert's *Die Winterreise*, sung to the hilt spiritually and musically by a good baritone.

A Viennese composer, talking about death.

Doubly moving.

You can make music in Munich.

Munich is the German threshold to Austria's love of music.

20 December

Art for art's sake, a sin in the Germanic sense of art.

Politics is being forged in the streets.

The street is characteristic of decaying civilization.

Am I going astray?

I see no stars now.

23 December

Off in the mountains. The white cloud light greets me from far away.

The window of my room opens to the giants. In the morning I stand, gazing up to them, humble and full of awe.

Giants!

Make my thoughts your peers.

Make them grow and grow until they attain your gigantic grandeur.

24 December
That was my yearning: for all the divine solitude and calm of the mountains, for white, virginal snow.

I was weary of the big city.

I am at home again in the mountains. I spend many hours in their white unspoiledness and find myself again.

25 December
Hertha Holk lights the Christmas tree. I think of home.

Old Yule songs.

I almost feel a longing for a lost Fatherland.

We exchange presents. A lovely old testament of Jesus from Hertha Holk is my greatest joy.

I thank her for my comfort and my strength.

29 December
We destroy ourselves squabbling.

A walk through the clear, cold, starry night. Mist rising from the earth.

Blissful wandering!

Mute, silent, close to the spirit of the world.

The wind sings in the trees.

The ancient song of the earth.

30 December
Oh, you mountains! Stone towers!

31 December
Year's end! I sum up.

An examination of my conscience and a request to the mind for progress and maturity.

I have grown stronger mentally and am aspiring toward clearer insights and more solid faith.

I know that beyond the spirit I shall find redemption in something I do not as yet know. I see clearly, but I am not yet

mature enough to orient my life according to knowledge.
Life is hard.
But we must overcome and make ourselves useful.
I love Hertha Holk and feel more deeply united with her day after day.

We must all be redeemed eventually.
The world pulls us with a thousand ties. We fail because of indifference and leniency, thus heaping our own guilt upon the ancient guilt we have inherited.
Guilt and atonement will lead to the new German man.

Twelve o'clock is striking outside.
We hold hands, each of us wishing the other what we consider the things most worth striving for in our own lives.
Hertha Holk's wish for me:
"To become a man who strikes a blow for the Fatherland."

As we pour the lead, my symbol for the new year is an eagle with widespread pinions.

We sit up until late at night.
Hertha Holk pours out all the wealth of her soul.

2 January
Snow in the mountains.

4 January
    I dreamed
    About you:
    You lay at my side,
    The pale moon playing around your left hand,
    And your hand was as white as snow.
    Your right hand lay on your heart,
    Rising and falling
    As your breast rose and fell.
    And as I lay there, striving with you,
    I heard you
    Desperately calling my name,

Very softly, as if you were making a request,
And a feeling of pain overcame me,
Melancholy and both pleasure and torment.
As if summoned by you, I stood up,
Knelt before your bed,
Buried my head in your breast,
And kissed your white hand.

15 January

I hear the string quartet play the Jahreszeiten.

Quartet of the four temperaments; and now they start to tell their tales.

The cello makes a statement. Theme!

The first violin caricatures this statement. And now they all pounce upon it. Argument, squabbling, four-way struggle; each seems to stick to his beat, one slips out unexpectedly, they laugh and make fun of him; he defends himself, becomes earnest, weeps, sobs, all of them weep along, they are so deeply touched, and they realize they have talked past one another. Take my hand. Friendship!

Now they chat a little in blissful harmony and then go home—a string quartet by Mozart.

Beethoven's final quartets: revelation of the end.

One feels Pan, one gropes in infinity, one stands at the doorway to eternity and timidly knocks in order to be let in.

I wandered among stars.

16 January

The street! I cannot get away from it. I am split into bits.

Politics! One is drawn into the maelstrom.

We Germans have always done too little politicking. Perhaps that is why we lost the war. We see politics only as a science, or, at best, a profession, but never as something concerning the entire nation.

Politics is anxiety about bread. Bread is not given by God; it is fought for and defended.

Give us this day our daily bread. No, give us your blessing on our bread, so that we may build and conquer today and always.

You call it materialism when we worry about bread? No,

never! This is the most primitive form of practical idealism. There is a difference between worrying about the simplest necessities of life and gathering gold and treasures.

Out in the streets, long processions of poor, pale, careworn people are demonstrating. Bread! Bread!

Do you call this patriotism—shooting them down like mad dogs?

Our nation has been forced into a yoke. The master race must drudge like slaves. Up and down, up and down.

The entire nation must form a united front against that: From the top to the bottom and from the bottom to the top.

That is the horror of it: A wall of arrogance, property, and education stands between the upper and lower classes. We no longer understand one another. We are not a nation, we are two partisan camps embroiled in a fierce feud. That is why we became a plaything in the hands of the powers that rule the world. When upper and lower classes are one, the earth will be ours.

But we shall never attain that goal through speeches and revolutions. A holy tempest must sweep us there.

We must start from scratch.

Some will brandish the flag, clutch the sword of hatred and love, and clear the way.

With the word in which the deed is already rearing.

Love live the republic!

That is what they are shouting outside. What do we care about the republic? Long live Germany! Long live its future!

Some day we shall have to account for ourselves before the tribunal of history. The question will not be: "Did you defend the Republic?" but "Where is the Reich? Where did you leave your Germany?"

Ivan Vienurovsky is my demon.
Hertha Holk does not understand my torment.
I must tear down and rebuild.
Down to the last stone.
I find no solution. I despair.

18 January

Hertha Holk causes me torments upon torments.

22 January

"Ivan Vienurovsky, you want to steal my final possession, the Fatherland. You will turn me into a beggar."

"Those are only transitional pains. I want to train you to have the courage for the ultimate struggle."

"I despair."

"The world is what makes us despair."

I shall not survive.

"So many people have said that, and so few were telling the truth."

"You are a devil."

"The devil is merely a fallen angel."

"I hate you."

"That does not matter, I shall not release you, Michael."

"Why did you select me?"

"You are pure and enthusiastic. You are a hope for us."

"I beg you, leave me alone. I want to find my way by myself."

"You are still trapped in old vestiges; your routes are too circuitous. You are wasting too much of my time."

"So you want me to stop being what and who I am? I am to become your slave?"

"Yes!"

I stand up, he suddenly turns pale and instinctively steps back.

I no longer control myself, I punch him in the face.

Then I collapse in a chair, almost unconscious.

Ivan Vienurovsky remains mute.

Suddenly, he comes towards me, grabs my hand, and begs my forgiveness.

26 January

I despair.

I am losing myself and you, Hertha Holk!

28 January

I have not kept my promise to Christ.

31 January

"Hertha Holk, you refuse to understand me!"

"I cannot understand you."

"Then we shall lose one another."

"I have not yet given up hope."

"Everything is burning out in me."

"Because you burn with other fires."

"I cannot help it."

"You must try, you will then find yourself again."

"You must not leave me."

"I will not leave you if you do not leave yourself."

5 February

The city and the people disgust me; I am degenerating here. I think I am ill.

My brain and my heart are throbbing and hammering.

Will no one help me?

I read the Bible. But I find no solution here either.

10 February

Away from people, escape to myself!

I am perishing here.

15 February

To the mountains! To the gods!

I must find myself.

Abandon everything. Cities, people, the world.

See nothing more, hear nothing more!

Stay alone in my loneliness!

18 February

I want to seek here!

Snow and eternity!

Mountains, friends!

You giant, you are my god!

You loom in majestic isolation.

Light! Let there be light!

I softly drink peace into my shredded heart.

Now I wish to work. Perhaps it will comfort me.

20 February

Prologue to *Christ*. Poet and world-spirit in the desert outside the world.

Poet:
    The spirit is always only one,
    Spirit united us,
    Spirit brings together those of good will.
    It suffers now and is ill;
    But in the final struggle
    It will pull the strong together.
    Spirit is God!
    I believe in God.
    When everything collapses, we shall grab
    The last plank
    From the safe port
    We watch
    The godless society
    Of old, holy Europe
    Collapse.
    The play begins.

27 February

Work redeems.
I am ashamed of my meager courage.

The third act of the *Christ Fantasy* is completed.
I have not yet spoken my last word.
But I find the redeeming word.

6 March

I wish to be a pioneer.
I wish to serve the Fatherland.
Pave the way.

10 March

I think about you a great deal; I believe in you. I cannot believe that you are lost to humanity. You are no deserter!

You shall not get rid of the demon until you turn him into a god.

We live in order to sacrifice.

Ivan Vienurovsky

16 March

My life consists only of suffering for your sake. You give me the bitterest things to taste. How unhappy I am about all the disquiet exhaled by your letters. I sense terrible things, but can do nothing. I must wait. That is the worst part of it. Why do we no longer understand one another? Is it my fault that I am as I am?

I have no choice, do you hear, I cannot do otherwise. I love you tremendously. That is why I suffer so much for your sake. When you despair, then I must despair with you, and then I have nothing I can hold on to.

Hertha Holk

22 March

My pen has wings. Everything in me is one single dramatic thought.

30 March

Christ died, Christ lives! I have seen him anew. As he is. Now I have said everything.

Five acts are on paper. I am finished.

4 April

Epilogue to *Christ*. Poet and world-spirit in the desert behind the world.

Poet:

I have been blessed,
The torment vanishes within me.
I awake,
I love, I believe!
Mighty word, you redeemer of my torment,
I clutch you with my hands
And shape you into the radiant

Beacon of the era.
I stand up, I have strength
To waken the dead.
They awaken from deep sleep,
At first only a few, then more and more.
The ranks fill up, an army arises,
A nation, a community.
Thought binds us,
We are united in faith,
In powerful will
For young form and wealth of promise,
And thus we shall give shape to the new Reich.

10 April
  The last of rest; then back to life.
  Everlasting struggle!
  I feel strong enough again to wage it.

15 April
  Munich!
  I plunge into the maelstrom of people.

  A letter from Hertha Holk lies on my table.
  "We must separate. Farewell! The torment became unbear-
able for me.
  "I weep for you, farewell."

  I dash to her apartment.
  "Fräulein Holk left Munich three days ago."
  "Where did she go?"
  "Nobody knows."

  I rage, I despair!
  I have to get out of here.
  Rain smashes into my face.
  Solitude.
  Life is bitter.
  I am doomed to remain alone. I destroy myself with others.
  I am one of those who shall remain alone.

I walk slowly through mud and water. Passersby laugh at me.
I can no longer push and shove.
I was young; my dream is over.

I come home late at night. I cannot eat.
Many white pages lie on my table. My play.
I hurl it into the corner. The shreds fly.
I look for a certain page.
I find it.
It is page two.
"Dedicated to Hertha Holk."
And now I am very petty.
I put the page into the stove. It burns, a red, glowing flame.
I stand and stare into the flame.
Life is always the same.
Yes, stubbornness, she would now say, stubbornness, stub-
bornness! That is why I am as I am, that is the only reason.
Tears come to my eyes. Oh, you cowardly soul!
I laugh at myself.
Then I rage again, hatred, anger, fury! I bang on the walls, I
punch myself.
I curse life.
I hate Ivan Vienurovsky.
I am no longer conscious.
I kiss Hertha Holk's portrait a thousand times. I act like a
child and I am not ashamed.
Then I tear up the picture and throw it into the flames.
I am infinitely tired, yet I cannot sleep.
I would like to scream, shriek like an animal.

I have lost everything!

20 April
Hertha Holk's final letter.

Michael,
I use your dear name. I would like to insert into this
name all my suffering for you and all my goodness. It is
late in the evening now.

I am very unhappy because I feel that you were the first and last man who loved me as I wanted to be loved and as I must be loved in order to be happy. Now I have lost everything. I have burned my bridges behind me, and I weep for nights on end for my great loss.

Let me visit you once again and pour out my heart to you. You must not think that I have changed, I am still the same Hertha Holk, and no one else, but I am now immeasurably unhappy. Whatever I do, I do the wrong thing; I almost feel as if life were no longer worth living.

Why have our paths gone in separate directions? Certainly our different spiritual developments have alienated us from each other. Before Munich, you were a man whose every emotion, no matter how subtle, I totally understood. Every hour you gave me more than all other people put together.

When you developed your new attitude, I suddenly began to doubt you, especially your love for me. My faith began to falter.

We women cannot live without faith in a man.

My heart still belonged to you for a long time, and none of my thoughts was concealed from you; nor was my concern about you. Then you went away. I wanted to speak to you, but I could not because I loved you far too much, perhaps also because I feared I would lose your love, in which I was already despairing so deeply. So I remained behind in torment and disintegration. Only then did I realize how deeply involved with you I am.

Never shall I forget the bitter, sleepless nights I suffered because of you. I disintegrated day after day, despairing more and more, and all my prayers to God for clarity and peace of mind remained unheeded. I was helpless, abandoned, alone in a storm of thoughts.

Your letters exhaled the same spirit of torment and disintegration. With you, I could not find the peace I needed. After all, you yourself were a seeker, a groping seeker. We women need something to hold onto. You did not offer me that. I yearned for peace of mind, and I knew I would never find it with you.

You ferment, you are filled with disquiet. I had to despair. I would perish with you. You know me, you also know that I (it is the bane of my existence) can never forget you. Now I would like to come to you and tell you how everything happened and what everything is like to-day—but I cannot, I must not.

Our souls have lost one another. They shall have to seek forever.

Hertha Holk

23 April

I write to Hertha Holk for the last time.

You have managed, Hertha Holk, to write me one last time, explaining everything that should have been said months ago. But it is good that you have said it. A word at the right time clears the air.

We have let go of one another. It had to be. We fulfilled each other as much as possible. That was our fate.

Why did you have to take everything from me when you left: both faith and hope? An idle question! I wanted to conquer life for you. You did not understand me. Perhaps you could not understand me. You resented my taking a different path. You believed my *Sturm und Drang* was terrible. You did not realize that my ways were not only new and accessible, but also higher than the ways of the golden means. I wanted to arouse something new in you and in me, something that I cannot articulate as yet. You could not wait. You saw only revolution instead of torment and beginning. I did what I had to do.

I will have to love you even beyond death.

Why did I become so inconsolable upon losing you? But I did not depair. I shall bring my law within me to fulfill-ment. Our era will be fulfilled in me.

Your beautiful hand has grown cold for me. And so too I believe my hands shall also grow cold some day and my heart shall stop beating. Who knows when? No sooner and no later than the law allows.

I shall keep seeking. I must find the road to salvation. I know that you shall bless my footsteps.

27 April

I walk through an alien city, torn along by a flood of people, not knowing where it comes from or where it is going to. My mind is blank, I just keep walking and walking, towards a goal I do not know.

I sit in a room I have never seen. Among people who are alien to me. Poor, careworn people. Workers, soldiers, officers, students. This is the German nation after the war. One sees old, threadbare uniforms, the dirty, tattered tunics bear the grieving signs of the Great War. I see all this as if in a dream.

I barely notice someone who suddenly stands in front of the room and begins to speak. Timid and faltering at first, as if seeking words for things that are too great to be squeezed into narrow forms.

Then, all at once, the flow of his speech is unleashed. I am captured, I perk up my ears. The man is gaining tempo. He seems illuminated.

Honor? Work? The flag? What do I hear? Do these concepts still exist in this nation, from which God has withdrawn his blessing hand?

The people here start to glow. Rays of hope beam on the gray, ragged faces. Someone stands up and raises his clenched fist. For the man next to him, his gray collar is too tight. Sweat is on his forehead; he wipes it off on his coatsleeve.

Two seats to my left sits an old officer, weeping like a child. I feel hot and cold.

I do not know what is happening inside me. I suddenly feel as if I could hear the thundering of cannons. Almost in a fog, I see that a few soldiers suddenly stand up and shout, "Hurray!" No one pays any attention to them.

The man on the podium is speaking. Rolling stone upon stone in a cathedral of the future. Everything that has been living in me for years is now taking shape, tangible form.

Revelation! Revelation!

Amid the ruins, someone is standing and raising the flag high.

All at once, the people around me are not strangers. They are all my brothers. The man over there, gray and threadbare, in his open military coat, smiles at me. "Comrade!" he says, quite unmotivated.

I feel compelled to leap up and shout: "We are all comrades. We must stand together!"

I can barely control myself.

I walk—nay, I am driven to the podium. I stand there for a long time, peering into the face of this individual.

He is no speaker. He is a prophet!

Sweat pours from his forehead. Two glowing eyes flash lightning in this gray, pale face. His fists are clenched.

Word upon word, sentence upon sentence boom like the Last Judgment.

I no longer know what I am doing.

I am beside myself.

I shout, "Hurray!" No one is surprised.

The man on the podium gazes at me for a moment. Those blue eyes strike me like flaming rays. This is a command!

I am reborn as of that moment.

Everything falls off me like slag.

I know my direction. The path of maturation.

I hear nothing now. I am intoxicated.

Suddenly I stand up; I climb on a chair, loom above that man, and shout, "Comrades! Freedom!"

I do not know what happened after that.

All I know is that I placed my hand in a man's throbbing hand. It was an oath for life. And my eyes sank into two large, blue stars.

28 April

I do not want to see you anymore until I am struck by God's ray.

29 April

I am sick of Munich now.

I have gone through too much here.

I must go to a different city.

Richard has asked me to come to Heidelberg. I am undecided.

30 April

I am leaving tomorrow. For Heidelberg!

It does not matter where one is, after all.

I take leave of no one here.

I run into Agnes Stahl on the street.

I can tell by the way she looks at me that she knows everything.

"When are you leaving?"

"Tomorrow."

"Farewell!"

She has tears in her eyes.

I know that Ivan Vienurovsky is waiting for me. But I do not visit him. I write my last letter in Munich to my mother.

Revolution is churning in me!

I have lost much and gained much.

I forge ahead to the highest law: Thou shalt be a sacrifice.

Sacrifice oneself to others! For one's neighbor!

I want to begin my path to self-sacrifice.

* * * * *

5 May

"I have come to Heidelberg to start all over again."

"You are stubbornly sinking into your solitude. You are learning to love it.

"You are becoming an eccentric."

"I have gone through a great deal, and I still have to digest a lot of it."

"You should start working here, Michael."

"Prepare for my examination?"

"Yes, you have to compromise. . . ."

"I cannot. I am confused by the whole so-called intellectual workings of the universities. I cannot see my way through.

"I cannot treat ideas as a business or a profession. They are more, infinitely more.

"Profession is a peripheral matter. We are healthy, after all.

"I can still earn a living."

"With the work of your hands?"

"Why not? Any profession, any job is what you make of it. We have to be retrained in this aspect too.

"We always talk so grandly about the ethical value of work. Why should we be too good for the work with which millions earn their livelihood?

"We are not yet courageous enough to go all the way. But perhaps some day work will be our salvation."

"That is ridiculous."

"We laugh at anything we do not understand. I want to pave the way here too. Just give me time!

"We have to wait until everything is ripe in us."

"You are very gifted, you can achieve something in the intellectual area."

"But I want to do something more than achieve something. I want to make, work, create. I want to pave the way into a different future.

"There have to be people among us who make examples of themselves.

"You can see for yourself how poor and wretched our universities look. All young talents are drained here.

"Future leaders of the people! This phrase is so often repeated.

"Just look. Today's leaders have emerged from their ranks. Or what are known as leaders: dwarfs instead of men!

"There are people who have learned nothing from the war. They think everything has to continue as before. Very few have an inkling of the new German type, who knows how to turn our material misery into an historical phenomenon.

"This has nothing to do with rebellion. This is a revolution! An upheaval, a new beginning, an assault on old altars.

"The war showed *ad absurdum* how deeply we have sunk. Two and a half million Germans were sacrificed without knowing why. We must atone for that today.

"I want to redeem.

"And if I go all the way, I have to form anew; and form myself anew as well."

Richard and I are standing at the Goethe Stone on the castle mountain, gazing down into this lovely town on the Neckar; Heidelberg lies below us in the fragrance of blossoms. A delicious May afternoon.

The sun shines over the town.

A fine smoke curls up from the chimneys, rising lazily into the air.

We can see very clearly into the distance, where a large city with its houses and towers closes off the landscape.

8 May

I stand in front of the castle and gaze up at the powerful, masculine splendor of this unique Renaissance structure.

How strange: One gradually forgets how to notice details, one barely sees them anymore. I look only for totality, essence, in both great and small things.

For me, the castle is a red monument of tamed energy.

We must return to reality, to ability, to concentrated labor and achievement.

I often think of Hertha Holk. Sometimes I almost despair.

We must take the powerful experiences of our time and tame them in a new, grand form.

Discipline and concentration are what we need. We must

reshape the torment of our lives into a factor that gives shape to life.

The wound of our time is lack of discipline. We all suffer from it.

We have to orient our dissipated energies towards a new, great goal.

We young people should not only demand, we must also accomplish.

Many of our modern talents are like mathematicians. If you take away their axiom, then the formula no longer works. Their entire ideology collapses like a house of cards.

They shape with their brains and not their hearts. They do too much of a good thing. They always risk becoming ridiculous and boring.

I do not work, because I do not as yet have a goal.

I am oppressed and unhappy.

13 May

How lamentable is this time! Disintegration and dissolution everywhere. No construction, no beginning, no forging ahead.

May blossoms here in lavish profusion. A multi-colored splendor, numbing the mind and senses.

A walk down the Neckar. On both sides, charming, green hills in their Sunday best.

15 May

I suffer for a poor, errant, lost nation.

But we still have strength left.

There is a man who knows the way.

I wish to become worthy of him.

17 May

Heidelberg!

People walk through the streets. Foreigners and honeymooners. Dozens of people ask how to get to the castle.

A baker's lad loudly and impudently whistles "Old Heidelberg, you fine town" through the hot afternoon.

Coaches drive lazily. The coachmen lecture the tourists.

Students in colorful caps, with great exuberance on their faces. They walk along the main street, self-important, with their noses in the air.

Fraternity whistles resound. Windows open upstairs, tavern jackets, boyish faces.

Ludwigsplatz is empty.

In front of a bookstore, a male student jokes around with a female student.

I have no desire to attend a lecture. I sit by the Neckar until evening. Then I go home, weary and brooding.

Richard is waiting for me. He brings me political articles and speeches. I am deeply disgusted at the thought of them.

I do not wish to offend him, so I promise to read them.

"This is the modern spirit."

"Yes, so far as it can reach the public, it has been tamed and tempered. The rest remains concealed.

"People do not care to learn about it."

"But we live in a revolutionary era, which is transvaluating all values. The modern spirit is breaking through in all things."

"That is easily said. Only cowardice and betrayal have broken through. Honor and strength lie buried. If the former is modern and the latter reactionary, then I am glad to be un-modern. Your revolution was no revolution. It only smashed forms; it did not change any contents. You run up a new flag, you supply a different name for the same firm, and that is all. What you dare serve up as revolution is an historical scandal.

"Whenever a true revolution shook history, it always had the same beacon at its very start: Armed conflict!

"You began by surrendering.

"Your state—or what you call a state—makes that obvious."

"We fought the revolution of pacifism. For the first time in history we began by laying down our arms. The others will have to follow suit; it cannot happen overnight."

"How naive to think that stupidity is contagious. You have long since gotten the slaps that you deserved from those others.

"But not only that: None of you still has the right to talk about socialism. You bartered socialism for cash loans, and the contracts you signed were death certificates for the socialist salvation.

"I am not against revolution. On the contrary! But I hated the cowardly revolt whose only goal is to overthrow cowards and bring other cowards to power.

"Over there lies France, our common enemy. Its negro armies are on the Rhine. You want to debate them away; throw down your arms and wait for the conscience of the world."

"What should we have done?"

"Proclaim resistance. If you cared so little for the nation that you did not even wish to risk your lives for it, then you should have put your bodies on the line against socialism, which was threatening the entire world, to the extent that it was genuine."

"Socialism is a doctrine of peace."

"That is stupid and illogical rhetoric. Anything worthwhile is threatened by worthlessness. That is why worthwhile things have to be defended. Including socialism. But the kind you want is worthless."

"Work and war are things that do not fit together."

"Wrong! Work is war! The great four-year struggle was a war *for* work. Work against money! Bread against money! You did not end that war. You merely placed it on a different level.

"When they saw that they could not force us, the soldiers of work, to our knees, they shot us down with poison arrows. And while the gray-garbed heroes, lethally wounded, sank to the ground, you people stood on their bodies and shouted: "Long live the republic!""

"We liberated labor from the yoke of capital."

"So much talk, so much nonsense. You released labor from the control of the industrial kings and forced it into the worse serfdom of money. That was your entire much-lauded revolution.

"To put it tritely: The business barons were replaced by the money barons. And that was all!"

"If we had resisted, there would have been senseless bloodshed."

"Oh, you mongers of claptrap! Bloodshed is never senseless, even if there is no visible success. The new order would have commenced with courage instead of cowardice. We would have remained a nation, a nation in crisis. But today, we are two fragments of a nation, and the slavedrivers of the world are cracking their whips over us."

"But we Germans will get together again little by little."

"Never! Not like this! You people are marked by destiny. The mark of Cain, the mark of fratricide, burns upon your foreheads. You people must be smashed if Germany is to live."

"You are arrogant."

"Yes, I am arrogant towards the soldiers of fortune who have caused our misfortune. I refuse any reconciliation with the new situation. For this new situation is actually old and dead. You should devour it until you choke."

"You are getting crude."

"Crudeness can only be answered with crudeness."

We fought for a long time until he, too, became heated. We no longer understand one another.

26 May

The landscape around Heidelberg is graceful and charming. A round chain of harmonious hills. A delight to the eyes.

I love walking down the Neckar as far as Neckar-Gmünd.

The long, lovely road runs past blossoming gardens.

29 May

I am not doing the right thing by God. But I have no courage as yet. I shall wait until I can do nothing more.

Sometimes I sit in the reading rooms, reading piles of newspapers and pursuing politics.

So many things are called "politics" today. When a profiteer uses the money stolen from us to buy a seat in the parliament, and then makes his deals with the people's money in the winding corridors of the parliament building—he is practicing politics.

Such are the parties of democracy: business groups! Nothing else. *Weltanschauung*? What kind of reactionary notion is that? Honor, loyalty, faith, conviction? Goodness, are you ever old-fashioned!

Left and right, right and left, a big tangle of corruption and shame. This heroic nation has developed a potbelly, which is worse than going to pot.

Parties thrive on unresolved issues. That is why they are not interested in resolving them.

This system is overripe for destruction.

Heads and fists must be revolutionized against it.

Right and left, thousands of people of the finest quality are standing. They must come together to take the destiny of the Fatherland in hand.

Politics of the people means making bread for the people.

Party politics means fighting for places at the feeding trough.

I want nothing to do with this kind of politics.

3 June

I am getting fed up with intellectual things. I am nauseated by every printed word. I find nothing in it that can save me.

Richard wants to help me with small means.

I can hardly say crude things to him.

Sometimes I sit around for hours, indolent and undecided, doing nothing, thinking nothing. Then again, I am haunted by a thousand devils, I forge plan upon plan.

But I do not begin to carry out any of them. Every evening I read the Sermon on the Mount. I find no solace in it, just despair and shame. Something is wrong.

In Germany's great schools, they are working hard, but doing little for the future. This is hack work.

We can never be saved by academic speculation!

7 June

If Christ could be brought back just as he was, he might redeem us.

10 June

Before me a new Fatherland arises.

I am learning how to love this Fatherland again. And the more humiliating its humiliation, the more ardent my ardor for it.

When I seek the new man, I first seek the German man.

I want to root myself in the soil of this Fatherland. This is the mother of my thoughts and yearnings.

We must not be blind to its faults and failings. But we want to love them too, because they are our faults and failings.

The new nationalism wants Germany's future, not the restoration of a shattered past.

What does nationalism mean: We support Germany because we are Germans, because Germany is our Fatherland, the German soul is our soul, because we are all a piece of the soul of Germany.

I hate the bigmouths who blab on and on about "Fatherland" and "patriotism."

Fatherland: This has to become something natural for us again.

All our German history is nothing but a constant chain of the struggle of the German soul against its adversaries.

The German soul is Faustian! It contains an instinctual drive towards work and its possibilities, and the eternal yearning for redemption by the spirit.

There is a German idea, just as there is a Russian idea. Some day, these two ideas will vie for the future.

15 June

Russia is a danger for us, we must overcome it. But we must get to know it if we are to overcome it.

Only now am I getting to see Ivan Vienurovsky in his heart of hearts.

He is a very unhappy man. He has been destroyed by Pan-Slavism.

I have not yet gotten the better of Ivan Vienurovsky.

The struggle raging through Europe today is a struggle between newly forming aristocratic strata.

Every era is shaped by aristocracies if it has historic rank.

Aristocracy = Rule by the best.

Nations never govern themselves. This madness was invented by liberalism. Its national sovereignty conceals the craftiest rascals, who do not want to be recognized.

As we can see, a cheap swindle; only a moron can be taken in by it.

The masses win: What madness! It is as if I said: Marble makes the sculpture. There is no art work without a creator! No nation without a statesman! No world without God!

History is a series of male decisions. It is not armies that win, but men with armies.

Europe will be reshaped by the nations that most quickly overcome mass madness and find their way back to the principle of the personality.

The new stratification of the aristocracy, however, will take place on the basis of new laws. Tradition will be replaced by achievement. The best! This title will be acquired, not inherited.

Geniuses are nothing but the highest expression of a nation's will. They are the incarnation of a creative national essence.

No oak grows without soil, roots, and strength. No man comes from nothingness. The nation is his soil, history his roots, blood his strength.

Great ideas are always pushed through by minorities. But ultimately, they create a condition to which whole nations owe their existence.

Works of art, inventions, ideas, battles, laws, and states— a man is always their alpha and omega.

Race is the breeding ground of all creative energy. Humanity is an exception. Reality is only the nation. Humanity is nothing but the multiplicity of nations. The nation is organic. Humanity has only become organic.

Being organic means having the ability to procreate organic life.

The forest is merely a multiplicity of trees.

I cannot wipe out nations and keep humanity alive just as I cannot destroy trees in order to spare the forest.

Trees in their totality are a forest.

Nations in their totality are humanity.

The stronger the oak becomes, the more beautifully it will adorn the forest.

The more comprehensively a nation is a nation, the more vividly it serves mankind. . . .

Everything else is devised, not naturally grown. That is why it does not hold out against history.

A minority of the best shall turn the German destiny.

We must therefore be braver, wiser, more radical, and have more character than the majority; we shall then triumph automatically.

We should not worry about the fact that other nations are ruled by scum. We have all the more prospect of winning in the end.

If the bravest hold the reins, they should openly say: We practice dictatorship, we assume the responsibility in the face of history—who shall cast the first stone at us?

If the cowards hold the reins, they say: The nation rules. They evade responsibility and stone anyone who comes out against this hypocrisy.

A minority shall always rule. The nation's only choice is to live under an open dictatorship of the bold or to die under a hypocritical democracy of cowards.

A calculation as simple as it is logical.

24 June

I put on my helmet, draw my sword and recite Liliencron.

Sometimes I have such an attack.

To be a soldier! Stand sentinel!

One must be a soldier forever.

A soldier serving the revolution of his nation.

I then think with horror of fire and devastation. I see the ruins of houses and villages smoldering in the evening light. Columns of fire climb into the air. Din and battle thunder.

I see broken eyes and hear the agonized moans of dying people.

My hands are black from powder fumes, my jacket is red with blood. No, war is not beautiful.

I hear loud orders, hurrahs. I join in: Hurrah, hurrah!

I am no longer human. I am overcome by a wild rage. I smell blood.

I shriek: "Advance! Advance!" I want to be a hero!

I shred my heart. What does a heart matter? I plunge into the torrent of fire.

I am a hero, a god, a redeemer.

I bleed. My arm hangs down, slack.

I have been hit.

I lose strength. I sink.

I black out.

I awaken from deep sleep. I lie alone in a vast, endless field.

The battle is over.

Cannons still boom in the distance.

The sky is high and strewn with lights. A red-hot glow far away.

I am shaken and stirred to the depths of my soul.

I barely feel my wound.

I am mute in the face of this grand experience.

This is war!

War! To the death!

As cruel as all life. I did not create it. I merely state that it is so.

And I imagine that the supreme being must have had his reasons for arranging things in this way and not some other way.

Eternal peace is a dream—it suffices for politics. The soldier can add: It is not even a beautiful dream.

All life is war.

The first act of civilization occurred when man forged the plow and the sword. The plow for peace, the sword for war.

Just as there can be no day without night, so too there can be no peace without war. One necessitates the other.

War and farmland, sword and plow—those are notions that belong together like man and woman.

The farmer sets his plow to the soil. Grain becomes bread. At the borders of the land stands the warrior, leaning upon his sword and keeping watch.

Farmer and warrior: Those are the soldiers for our daily bread.

That is how God made the world. It has always been like that, and so shall it always be.

26 June

Agnes Stahl writes me from Munich:

> I am coming to Heidelberg in the next few weeks; we shall then meet again. You are more fortunate than we since you see clearly and have courage. The courage of one's convictions—that is what it is called. You do not cling to life. Such a stance makes a man strong. Now that you are no longer here, I realize what a wealth of active strength you emanate.
>
> You owe it to youth not to despair.

No, I must not despair!

I must be brave!

"Until soon, Agnes Stahl."

Everything within me rebels against the intellect.

I am on the verge of the final departure.

2 July

"I will have to work, Agnes Stahl, that is my ultimate salvation."

"You have always worked."

"No, I was a visionary, an aesthete, a rhetorician.

"I wanted to redeem the world with rhetoric.

"I spared myself.

"Now I want to intervene in the course of things. One cannot remain neutral when two opponents, armed to the teeth, fight for the future."

"Two opponents? Where and when?"

"Yes, you others do not see anything, you do not want to see it. Nevertheless, it is so. Money has enslaved us, work shall set us free. With the political bourgeoisie, we reel into the abyss; with the political proletariat, we shall be resurrected."

"You are against the class struggle, yet you preach the rule of one class?"

"Workers are not a class. Class comes from economics. Workers have their roots in politics. They are an historical estate. A nation is important only if its ruling estate is something. The political bourgeoisie is nothing and wishes to be nothing. It only wants to live, live very primitively. That is why it is perishing.

"One can preserve life only if one is willing to die for it!

"The proletariat, in contrast, has to carry out a mission, especially for Germany. He has to free Germany inwardly and outwardly. That is a world mission. If Germany goes under, then the light of the world will go out."

"You are not very modest."

"Only scoundrels are modest. The less I demand for myself, the more passionately I struggle for the rights of my nation. And since I have seen these rights sold and huckstered away by the bourgeoisie, I shall make a clean break with the past and start all over again with work."

"You can revolutionize all you like. Fat always rises to the top."

"Of course, the fat people will always have their say; they will own their villas and give ceremonial speeches. Man as a broad mass dominates the day, today and tomorrow. But we shall carve our name into history. We alone!

"The others live today. That is why they shall be dead for the future. But those who renounce life today, they shall be alive tomorrow."

"Why renounce it? Who will thank you for it?"

"Thank? I do not know that word. I want no thanks. None of us want it. We want to make history. Who cares about a little life?"

"But you yourself come from the bourgeoisie."

"I have learned to hate it all the more intensely. One must go through something to learn to love it completely or hate it completely.

"I hate the burgher because he is a coward and refuses to fight. He is only a zoological creature, that is all.

"Soldiers, students, and workers shall build the new Reich. I was a soldier, I am a student, I want to be a worker. I must go through all three levels in order to show the way. I was forbidden to speak, so I shall begin to act. Each man in his place."

"You love sacrifices?"

"Yes, one must sacrifice. I do not love it, but I have to do it. I must climb down into the deepest depth. We must begin from below.

"So far, we have been heirs. We gratefully accepted what was handed down to us.

"We must start all over again.

"I want to be ruthless and commit myself entirely."

"You have always committed yourself totally. You were pure ardor and devotion."

"But for the wrong things. The new German will be born in workshops, not in books.

"We have written enough, we have blithered and blathered enough. Now we must work."

"You will perish in the attempt."

"No, I shall live.

"I shall make a start."

"Work shall degrade you into a serf."

"No, I shall ennoble work.

"Work is not a thing in itself, it is merely a step upward."

"You shame us all."

"I have no special merit. This is what I must be and do."

We remain silent for a long time. It is late, and the day is fading out.

8 July

I am returning to Russia and taking along my memory of you as hope and bitterness. Some day we may have to cross swords again; if not we ourselves, then our ideas. We are not yet done with each other. Your world and my world must once again fight for the ultimate form of existence. Shall the synthesis be found? I would like to hope so but I can barely believe it. One cannot change nature. Her oldest law is struggle.

Very well then, struggle! But a struggle with honest weapons!

So I shall pull off my mask and show you my true face: I am a Russian!

I want Russia to bring in the new world. Rome is finished. The new big R is: Russia. Farewell!

Agnes Stahl tells me that you are working, that you want to start from below. I know you well enough to know that you shall carry out your resolutions. You are making a surprising move. I shall need time to parry.

You are arming yourself quickly; you wage your struggle instinctively, I wage it consciously.

For me, you are German youth about to redeem itself. You are strong, but we shall be stronger.

Ivan Vienurovsky

So I am rid of you, Ivan Vienurovsky!

I know what I have to do.

Without meaning to, you have shown me the way. I shall find salvation.

Yes, we shall cross swords, the German and the Russian.

Teuton and Slav!

12 July

A hopelessness overwhelms me with elemental power.

I hate this gentle Heidelberg!

Restlessness! Yearning!

I need work.

I cannot stand being with dead books anymore.

I want to give shape. More than intellect operates within us. We must reshape work.

Intellect is lifeless. It cannot fill out an existence.

I want to do the first deed. Uncompromisingly.

How can one write books and gather knowledge when Germany lies in rubble? Should not man and woman, old and young, lend a hand in the labor of freedom?

Where are the soldiers of the war? They draw up payrolls, buy and sell wares, do commerce and work, bring children into the world—and the Fatherland is going to the dogs. Where will it end?

Germany is a money province, burdened with treaties that would have never been forced upon an African tribe; statesmen at the helm, saying yes and negotiating away things that do not belong to them.

Soldiers! Soldiers!

Workers! Workers!

Where is the spirit that did not collapse at Verdun?

Smash cowardice to bits!
I do not want to despair!
In my mind's eye, I see legions marching.
Money be damned!

17 July
I seek connections and wander through chaos.

Strike me dead, we are doomed!
We are astray! What shall we do?
We are chosen by the devil!
And now he leads us by our noses.

26 July
I have reached my goal. My soul is still.
The semester is over. So much for lecture halls and book
dust.
I have written to my mother. My mind is set:
I shall go down into the mine, I shall be a miner!
The least among the poor!
I want to work. Set an example.
Save myself; pave the way for others.
To salvation through sacrifice!

4 August
A few days at home!
The old village, my house, the lower Rhine!
Plain!
I walk through the fields before sunrise. Fog brews over the
land. It is still quite silent.
I walk, walk as in a dream.
Slender birches stand individually in rows.
Sun struggles with black and gray.
I walk through lonesome fields.
A heavy smell comes from the soil. The smell of the earth.
The earth steams; the field is giving birth. Fruit is rising.
Holy hour of creation!
A lark rises. *Tirili!* Then a second.
Light swells. A sea glows.

The sun ascends. Glowing red, blood red. The land lies in gold.

Home! Earth! Mother!

One sees houses in the distance, villages, sharp steeples.
The fog rises.
The birches begin to shine.
I walk through damp meadows.

You are not flashy, my home. You do not shine in Sunday best, you do not drape the purple cloak of beauty over your shoulders.

You are modest, earth of my homeland! But the harvest buds lie inside your soil. You bring fruit to its fullness.

Our eyes roam far across your plains. We can see all the way to the horizon.

Your people are loyal and hardworking, silent during the day and full of living joy when it is time to rest in the evening.

Chimneys smoke in the distance. Work is beginning in the towns.

Farmland and factory are intertwined.

I come from you, homeland! I remain in you!
You give me strength and life!
I thrust my roots deeper into you.

7 August

I say goodbye to my mother. A quiet, earnest moment.
We sit at the hearth in the large kitchen.
"I know you want to do what's right, that is why I bless your decision."
"We must do something, Mother, otherwise life will devour us. We must not stand still."
"You will suffer a great deal and have to overcome even more. But I have faith in you."
"I am not led by vanity and surfeit. I must, I have no choice. I do not wish to be an heir. I want to begin for myself, start from below.

"After all, I shall work not for the sake of work, but for salvation."

"This path shall bring suffering to you and us. You go there because you feel you are strong enough. I do not doubt that you shall see it through."

"I take along all strength from my homeland. I am strong because I have roots."

"Say no more. I know what you have gone through."

"One can say so little when one has seen so much. I have not yet dealt with it fully."

"Well then, God be with you! Trust in Him! You cannot do everything with your own strength. He will have to help you in the end.

"There shall come a time when you shall stand all alone. Make sure you still have Him. Do not forget to pray!

"Everyone prays in his own way. Work, too, is prayer."

"Farewell, Mother!"

She stands for a moment, irresolute, timid. I see tears running down her old, hollow cheeks.

I feel as if my heart must break.

And then I kiss her dear, work-worn hands for the last time.

10 August

Noise welcomes me. Steam and work!

A whole land in furious creation.

Work!

The town is gray and wretched. The houses sooty, the people earnest and taciturn.

Black masses roll through the streets; narrow, pale faces over bent necks. Children sit begging on street corners.

In front of the shops, women stand with old, gray faces.

Evening is gathering. Arc lamps flare up. Light over filth and poverty.

My heart convulses.

Prostitutes and pimps trudge through narrow alleys.

Red lights burn here.

It is as though the evening were beating black wings over the town.

Wealth and poverty dwell here side by side.

I feel like weeping.

Haste and restlessness over everything here. Cars dashing. Time is money!

The lamps shine.

I am carried by the human torrent through wide and narrow streets.

I am tired, worn out.

My mind is blank.

I stand on a corner and peer into the black surging.

Drunks stagger past, singing and bawling.

A policeman stands there; serious, tall, and stern.

The sky gray. No stars shining.

One sees only smoke and distant fire.

A rain starts falling. The drops splash down slowly.

Wearily, lazily, into the filth.

I halt. The water runs down my cap.

I can go no further. My feet are rigid.

I stand on and on, until the din dies out, until the street is empty.

Dirty water turns to mud in the puddles.

Railroad trains roll in the distance.

Their thunderous clatter dies out far in the night.

14 August

My first descent!

I climb into the lowering cage. I fall, I plunge—for only an instant. Then I stand on solid ground. There is still light around me.

The small mine lantern hangs on my chest.

I crawl through dark, narrow corridors. It seems to take days, months, years.

On and on! On and on! Through narrow holes, head first. Like a cat.

The path goes on forever.

My breath is still. The air is oppressively hot.

Sweat on my brow. I have no time to wipe it off.

My hands glow. They already ache. This is only the beginning.

On and on!

I am accompanied by a deputy. He crawls ahead of me. He does so naturally!

Sometimes he shouts back something. I do not understand him.

You cannot understand your own words here.

My ears roar and buzz.

I hear the banging of a thousand hammers. Din and screams around me. I feel as if I were about to black out.

This is madness!

My eyes ache. I see nothing now. Dust covers my face.

I crawl on. Finally we reach our goal.

The deputy instructs me in the black art. One hour. Two hours.

Then I am alone. And I start to bang.

The coal fragments fly down.

When I stop to think, I feel as if days have already flown by.

I look at my watch.

Only three hours since I descended!

I am infinitely tired.

My arms are lifeless. My hands bleed.

Back to work! I cannot get away. It holds me like a demon.

I hammer and hammer. I hit my hands. Unbearable pain!

The blood runs down my thumb and forefinger. I hold them in my mouth. They burn like fire.

Strike! Strike! The work whips me along. I am its servant, its slave, its dog!

I shall not stop until I collapse.

I feel like screaming.

I feel as if I were screaming, bellowing like a hungry beast.

Fire splashes from the stones. I strike flames! I strike light.

I am no longer a human being. I am a titan. A god!

The deputy kneels next to me. He holds my arm.

"That's what they're all like, the young men who come to us from the universities. The first day in the pit is intoxicating. That will pass.

"Half-hour food break. You have to eat something."

He addresses me in the familiar form. I would like to embrace him.

Yes, you are my brother. We are all brothers down here.

Do not hate me, do not be angry at me. I am one of you.

He gives me schnapps. I greedily drink two or three glasses. It runs down my throat like fire.

I cannot eat. Bread disgusts me.

Just drink, drink!

My throat is parched. Back to work!

I hammer for an eternity. The hours run slowly, indolently.

I am so tired. I long for the end of the shift.

At last! At last!

The hour I have longed for!

Up! Up!

The sun shines above. The day is bright.

The night is done! Day!

I have never greeted the day so ardently.

I am caked with filth. My hands are black and bloody.

My fingers stick together. My hair hangs disheveled over my forehead.

I am dead tired. Every part of me is in pain.

To the bath! Wash off the dirt and blood!

A human being! A human being again!

"Till tomorrow," the deputy shouts to me.

His name is Matthias Grützer. I shake his hand.

I would like to kiss it. How dear this hand is to me, this worker's hand!

I gaze after him for a long time.

Then I stagger out. As if drunk.

Through the sunshine!

Out here, it seems as if nothing had happened. As if it were yesterday!

The chimneys smoke. Steam, fumes, soot, flames against plain houses belonging to a miner's family.

Singing in the air.

The song of work!

I look for something green. I find nothing.

A tree, a bush, a flower.

Nothing! Everything gray! Short, as if shaven.

Only the towers, the chimneys, the poles, the stacks loom into the air.

I walk on, stagger on.

Faster, faster, and faster!

I start off to town; I dash, I whiz. I fly like the wind. I dash through the streets, out of the town.

Out! Out! Into the fields!

Everywhere towers, chimneys, poles, stacks!

Gray on gray and sunshine above it all.

Bright sunshine!

Am I crazy? Am I dreaming?

Has the world perished?

Are there no people left? Just animals, black beasts? Devils, pit devils?

But am I myself an animal, a black beast, a devil, a pit devil?

I am whipped by demons.

Someone inside of me observes me, someone else, a second person.

Relentlessly. Sharply. Critically.

Ivan Vienurovsky!

Now I've got you, you bastard!

You beast! You devil! You Satan!

Come here, I want to grab you. I want to grab you by the throat.

You won't get me! Never! Never!

We'll see who's stronger.

I laugh. I shout.

People come towards me, eye me quizzically, grin, talk, point at me.

I run on.

On and on!

To the ends of the earth!

I wrestle with Ivan Vienurovsky. He is as agile as a cat.

But I am stronger than he.

Now I grab him by the throat.

I hurl him to the ground.

There he lies!

His throat rattling, his eyes bloodshot.
Die, you dog!
I kick his skull in.
And now I am free!
The last tempter beaten down.
The poison is out.
I am free!
I remain! I remain!
I want to save myself. Redeem myself with my own strength.
I want to show the way, make a thrust, set an example.
I plunge to the ground and kiss earth. Hard, brown earth.
German earth!
Late that evening, I come home and fall lifeless on my bed.

20 August

I live outside the town, in the colony, in one of the small, plain houses that belongs to a miner's family.

My room is simple, poor. A bed, a chair, a table, washing utensils, and a wardrobe.

I have taken along two books. The Bible and *Faust*.

The noise of children fills the house. But I am not annoyed.

I like hearing children play, especially in the afternoon, when I come home from work.

Sometimes I sit in my room for a long time, listening to the loud screaming and shrieking of the children.

A straight road runs through the colony. To the left and right there are houses. All in straight lines. All identical. Simple, tasteless, but usually rather clean. The children play in the street. The children of poverty, with gray faces and earnest eyes.

Merriment does not dwell in our street.

Even the children here are not like children in other places.

One sees many disfigured and retarded children. They usually sit at the house doors rather than carry on with the other children. They watch the others play, they are earnest and taciturn.

Men are always standing outside the houses. They are between shifts, for the miners have different shifts.

They are earnest men of few words. As the children already are. Many of the men read newspapers. But morosely. Some are arguing.

I think I notice hostile eyes following me when I walk along the streets.

But I may be wrong.

Everything is so new and strange for me.

In any case, the people I live with are very gruff and grumpy with me.

I write no letters and receive no letters. No one knows where I am.

I am completely on my own.

During my free time, I sleep or I walk along the streets.

Up and down!

I think of nothing. I am neither cheery nor sad.

Nor can I claim to be happy. The hard works drains me. Sometimes I think I will collapse.

But then I grit my teeth and think about the torment of the past few months.

These memories help me along.

But I am immensely content when I come home from work.

The beginning remains equally hard every day.

I am now getting to understand things that once were alien and unfamiliar to me.

One must go through every depth at least once.

These are all merely steps towards life.

The workers' question becomes increasingly clear to me in all its tragic implications. One must feel it personally, physically. Bury all the capitalists in the world. We shall then have come a lot further.

What good does it do the worker to be right? He has to have power in order to get his rights.

Might always comes before right.

The workers are in the same relationship to money as Germany is to the world. No amount of lamenting helps. You or me! Either one person puts his heel on the other's neck or vice versa.

A community of the people? Yes indeed! When each individual has his rights. But like this? We should hold our tongues so that you out there can have your peace? Wouldn't you like that?!

A truce? The enemy always says that, but only after crossing the moat, entering the castle, and then sprawling around in the castle rooms, sneering and arrogant.

What do you mean: Let's get along? The person who broke the peace is the one who should restore it. Or else we will force him to do so.

My brother is only he who sees me as his brother.

How shattering! These people hate Germany because their love for Germany has been trod upon. Their hatred is merely unrequited, often-deceived love.

The man who risks his life for a country has acquired the right to share in its ownership. Life is equally sacred for both the master and the servant. Each can lose his life only once.

When these people ask, "What is Germany to us?" they sometimes sound more optimistic than when a national profiteer cries, *"Deutschland über alles!"*

We have a difficult task ahead of us, and it is made even harder by the thousand irresponsible omissions that we have to cope with. If we carry out our task—and we must carry it out—then Germany will reshape the world.

When these bowed heads are raised some day, when these weary eyes begin to flash some day, when these labor-hardened fists are clenched some day, when these pale, embittered mouths open up some day, when these millions of throats shout some day: "Down with the shame! The Fatherland belongs to the man who frees it! Where are our guns?"

Then the earth shall tremble before us.

What difference will a tiny life make in those circumstances?

26 August
The men in the pit hate me. They cause me trouble whenever they can. None of them ever talks to me.

Only the deputy Matthias Grützer says something to me now and then.

I do not know the reasons for their attitude. Perhaps they sense in me the master, the arrogant master. I can do nothing about that.

Perhaps they are right. I am not one of them. Not yet.

Nothing separates me as much from these people as my real or imagined intellectual arrogance. They do not believe me.

They seem to have been disappointed far too often.

That is the gist of the social issue. We can no longer communicate. Blood brothers are separated by property, they speak different languages and have different lifestyles.

We have become two fragments of one people. Above and below, in between a wall. This situation finds its sharpest expression in economy, but it affects all areas of living together. We are separated by everything that ought to bind us. One only gets to know this properly by experience.

If one of those phrase-mongers came down into the pit and prattled on about patriotism, they would merely treat him to a pitiful smile or probably beat him black and blue.

Socialism: the bridge from left to right, across which those who are willing to make sacrifices come together. There is a lot of riffraff on both sides, a mob. But there are several people with good minds in the lead. Only they shall find the solution.

I come from above and go below. I want to find comrades who will accompany me from below to above.

We shall form a bridge. Perhaps with our own formidable backs so that others will have a path.

So be it! This mission is worth the sacrifice of the best.

Someone comes to me today, grins at me, and says: "You must be one of those profiteers from above. You want to play the spy! Watch it! We work with dynamite here."

The blood shoots to my head. My hand trembles. I am about to punch the man in his neck.

All at once, I calm down. I gape at him and say: "You don't deserve getting punched. You don't know what you're doing."

He becomes embarrassed, steals off wordlessly, and murmurs with the others.

I know that he now hates my guts.

I will have to be careful.

2 September

The pit is a demon. It grabs me and will not let me go.

I am spellbound.

I can hardly wait until I go down again. I feel out of place up here, as if I had no proper place to claim.

As if I were needed below.

I now belong completely in the pit.

I am getting a full salary like the others. It is not much, but a single man can get along on it.

Besides, I need nothing else. I am on my own.

I live from the work of my hands.

I am my own boss!

How happy this work makes me!

One can see what one produces. One strikes coal out of the earth. One fights with the element, one forces precious treasures out of the ground.

One becomes proud and lonesome.

My hands are raw, covered with cracks from old and fresh wounds.

Several days ago, a falling rock knocked two of my teeth out.

When I look in the mirror, I barely recognize myself. My cheeks are sunken, my face is gray. Coal dust fills my eyebrows and the creases around my nose.

"You won't be able to wash it out, it will have to wear off some day," says Matthias Grützer.

There is a huge gap in my mouth. My lip is still swollen, suffused with blood.

But I feel fresh and healthy. I believe my strength is growing.

10 September

I get up every morning at four a.m. It is still dark.

I dress by candlelight. I dress quickly.

A cup of hot coffee, then out I go.

The pit is a long way off. It is almost forty-five minutes away.

We descend at five. I have to hurry.

The road is dark. The red glow in the distance shows me my

direction. I stumble over stones and shrubs. On and on!

It is still cold. Walking keeps you warm.

On and on!

Black shadows rise before me in the distance. Towers, chimneys.

I hear buzzing and singing.

A devil rides me, drives me along.

To the pit! To the pit!

I stride past meager farmland. I smell the beloved fragrance of the earth.

An animal, a dog, barks somewhere far away.

A miner's gray house at the roadside every so often. Light is on in a room. People are getting up to work.

The day rises, tired and leaden. Everything gray on gray. I shudder.

I must grit my teeth to keep from despairing.

A rooster crows. Greetings from my homeland!

Damned beast!

Just do not think.

The gates of the mine! In I go!

The descent!

There they sit, the old, the young, near the entrance. Their lamps on their chests, waiting.

They sit down each in turn. Mute, bleak.

One hears only an occasional word. Whispered.

I sit down behind the last one.

Good luck!

Two or three answer me grumpily.

We wait! Wait until the moment when we have to get to work. Yearning under a cruel, ruthless compulsion.

The earth draws us.

We are its slaves.

Damned slaves, carrying the hard yoke of labor on our necks. Silent, mute, affectless, joyless.

We do not think, we do not lament.

We carry!

We do not strive and we do not weep.

This is how it must be!

We carry the burden. For all others.

We carry!
Sun goes up. Light grows all around us. The day begins.
A second night for us.
The siren screams.
We climb into the cage and buzz into the depth.

15 September

I feel fine only when the pit is full of crashing and booming.
When the beams fly and the rocks split. When the din of work
clatters so loud that you cannot hear yourself think anymore.

Symphony of work!

Full, sated life!

Work! Create! Put your shoulder to the wheel!

Be the master! Conqueror! King of life!

And then again I yearn for the divine solitude of the mountains, and for untouched, white snow.

18 September

It is neither the mind nor work that sets us free. They are both
merely forms of a higher power.

Struggle is the be-all and end-all. I have taken up the struggle
with myself. First we must overcome our inner bastard and
force him to the ground. Everything else is then as easy as pie.

With mind, work, and struggle, we form the motor that will
set our era into motion.

It will be an age of the newly formed aristocracy of achievement.

20 September

Money is the bane of mankind. It nips greatness and goodness
in the bud. Sweat and blood adhere to every penny.

I hate Mammon.

He trains men for activity and sated relaxation. He poisons
our very works within us, making us servile to low, common in-
stincts.

The worst day of the week for me is payday. They throw the
money to us like bones to dogs.

This world is hard and cruel. As hard as money in the thin
hands of the miser.

Thrift is a sticky virtue.
Gather gold and treasures.
But I want to lavish myself out of the excess of my soul.

Money is the standard of value used by liberalism. This doctrine is so devoid of any soul that it managed to turn shadow into substance. That is why it is slowly perishing. Money is the bane of work.

One cannot prize money more than life. When one does, all noble strength runs dry.

Money is a means to an end, not an end in itself. If it becomes an end in itself, then it inevitably degrades work into a means to an end.

If a nation measures everything by money, then this nation is heading for its final, gray end. It will be slowly devoured by the disintegrating powers of gold, which have always wiped out nations and cultures.

While the soldiers of the Great War risked their lives to protect their homeland, and two million bled to death, the profiteers minted gold from the noble red fluid. Later, they used this gold to cheat the homecoming soldiers out of their homes.

Thus, the war was won by money and lost by work. Nations were neither winners nor losers. They only did the dirty work for money or defended work against such menial service.

Germany fought for work. France fought for money. Work lost. Money won.

Money makes the world go round! A dreadful statement when true. Today, we are being destroyed by its factuality. Money—Jew. The thing and the person, they belong together.

Money has no roots. It exists above the races. It gradually eats its way into the sound organisms of the nations, slowly poisoning their creative strength.

We must fight and work in order to free ourselves from money. We must smash the delusion within ourselves. Then the golden calf will some day collapse.

Liberalism is, in its deepest sense, the doctrine of money.

Liberalism means: I believe in Mammon.

Socialism means: I believe in work.

23 September

The children play in the narrow vestibule when I return from work.

I pick up one child, a little girl, and carry her to my room. She is embarrassed and begins to cry. I give her a sparkling stone which I have found down in the pit.

She begins to trust me and starts playing in my room.

"What's your name?"

"Anna."

"Anna, what a lovely name you have.

"Look, I found this stone down in the pit. I brought it back for you.

"Do you see the way it glows? If you held it in the sun, it would be a lot more beautiful. It would shine like a diamond."

"My father also works down in the pit. He's taking a nap now."

"Yes, your father and I, we both work down in the pit."

"Do all people work in mines?"

"No! But everyone must work. Some on the surface, the others under the surface. Some sow and reap the grain, so that we can have bread. The others get coal from the earth, so that we can have heat and light."

"Are there people who do not work?"

"Yes! But when we, the workers, stand together, we shall be able to deal with the idlers. The man who does not work should not eat."

A pause.

"My mother is in the kitchen, peeling potatoes."

"Yes, your mother works hard too. Do you like her?"

"Yes, but I don't like my father. He beats me."

"Doesn't your mother beat you?"

"No, Mother doesn't beat me. Mother is good."

The little girl grabs my hand and pulls me into the tiny, poor kitchen.

"Anna, stop that!"

"Oh, don't worry, she's so sweet."

"She'll bother you."

"No."

A long silence.
I return to my room, hesitant, and annoyed at myself.

25 September
I am beginning to gain prestige among my comrades.
Some of them occasionally exchange a word or two with me.
Their mistrust is slowly vanishing.
My landlord and landlady are becoming friendlier to me.
This afternoon, I found a few small, modest flowers on my table.
How delighted I was!
The children call out my name when they spot me, and they instantly grab my hands.

3 October
"You are destroying yourself, Michael, you will not be able to hold out. You are wiping yourself out."
"A man can endure more than one thinks. One simply should not spare oneself. One has to take on so much in life.
"In the war, we wrested a great deal more from our bodies and our defiance, yet we did not perish."
"But we did suffer deeply, both in our bodies and in our souls."
"You are right, Matthias, we will not get over that so easily. But you see, we all endured it together, the worker and the master.
"Out in the trenches, we lay side by side, the man from the mansion and the man from the miner's shack.
"We joined together, we became friends, we finally got to know one another.
"And when the war was over, that accursed gap opened up again.
"Work is war without cannons. When we work, we have to join together too, with the fist and the mind. We have to understand one another again, the sooner the better.
"Life is hard. We have no time to be enemies. We have to get bread for the millions who exist and for the millions who have not yet been born. Otherwise, we will collapse sooner or later."
"Yes, but no one up there thinks as you do. All they care

about is money and power."

"Then we must force those creatures to think otherwise. Some people are impressed only by a fist under their noses. We must be ruthless. We, the young, have the greater authority in history.

"The old still don't want to recognize that the young even exist. They will defend their power to the last.

"But some day, they shall lose. Ultimately, youth must win.

"We young men, we shall attack. The attacker is always stronger than the defender.

"Once we set ourselves free, we can also free the workers. And freed workers will release the Fatherland from its chains."

"What you say about work and war is true. And the best thing about it is that you yourself are making your own words come true.

"You do not mouth fancy phrases like other people. You act.

"The moment you came here, the first time I saw you, I knew that you were a pioneer of the idea of work.

"Ah, we see so many students here from the universities. They all work hard and do their duty down below.

"But most of them do not understand us miners. They come down to us. Or rather, they condescend. There is always some kind of gap between us and them. That is why there is such a brooding hatred between us and the whitehands.

"You will see a lot of hostility here towards the students. But I know you will do better. You do not want to come down to us, you want to bring us up to you.

"You know how to go about doing this because you see us as comrades. That is why you find the right words to open our hearts."

During breakfast, I kneel next to Matthias Grützer down in the tunnel. We speak at long intervals and we have to shout to make ourselves heard.

9 October

Passive resistance.

They do not want to give the miners more. They cannot live on what they earn.

They stand down in the tunnels, arguing, cursing. It is almost as silent here as on a holiday.

No one does a stroke of work.

We hear hate-filled threats, oaths, curses.

For a day now, my situation has been almost untenable. I am openly threatened. Imprecations whirl around my ears from all sides.

They suspect me of being a spy and a strike-breaker. They have already openly accused me of being in the pay of the capitalists.

Matthias Grützer is the only one to take my side.

17 October

Thousands of men are gathered outside the mine. Screams and songs, stones flying, threatening, clenched fists.

They wedge themselves in front of the management building.

Suddenly, a cry, a shout, a command. Panes clatter, a door is smashed in, then wild chaos. They roll in through the door like a vast torrent.

A woman with raised arms comes down the steps and, shrieking, comes towards the men. Instantly she lies under the raging mob and is trampled to the ground.

Everything within me is fight, convulsion, torment.

I plunge ahead, I desperately shout at the others: "This is madness!"

Shouts of "Strike-breaker! Spy! Paid agent!" in wild chaos.

Then I feel a punch in my head. Blood flows over my forehead and temples. I wipe it away with my hand. More and more blood!

I reel, I sink.

Then I black out.

When I awaken I am lying in my bed. Matthias Grützer stands watching over me.

I feel pounding and an unbearable pain up in my head.

I am endlessly tired.

Then I lose consciousness.

Today, I can think clearly about everything. However, I cannot forget the wild image of that evening.

They struck me down like an animal. They would not treat a dog in that way.

They simply struck me down! And I only wanted to help a defenseless woman.

I feel no anger, no resentment. They do not know me. Nor did they realize what I wanted to do. They are all so poor and helpless.

Theirs was an act of desperation.

But a thorn did remain in my soul.

25 October

Back into the pit for the first time!

I encounter good, friendly faces. They are considerate, almost tender to me.

An old miner comes to me and offers me his hard hand.

Good luck! How beautiful that sounds! A greeting for men who are chained together by a common misery.

Matthias Grützer has worked for me. He has enlightened them. I thank him.

During breakfast, a comrade comes towards me. He is coming on behalf of the others and asks me for forgiveness. I am embarrassed. I do not know what to say.

Matthias Grützer stands next to me.

And suddenly I feel my eyes getting wet and two thick tears running down my cheeks.

Yes, now we have found our ways to one another. Now I am at home among you.

I am no longer a stranger, no longer an intruder.

A worker among workers!

That is what I am, that is what I shall remain!

I am one of you. I have fought for and won the right to call this my home.

Blessed wound!

30 October

I stumble upon Vincent van Gogh again. How differently from that time in Munich. I no longer see the painter, I see the man, the God-seeker.

I use a bit of my salary to buy his poignant letters to his brother Theo.

The man is greater than the artist.

The old temples must be demolished so that we can build new ones!

2 November

I find Christ again.

The German quest for God is not to be separated from Christ.

We have lost our true cohesion with God. We are neither warm nor cold. Half Christian, half heathen. Yes, even the best are groping in the dark, not knowing what to do.

But here too, one must speak openly. A nation without religion is like a man without breath.

The various churches have failed. Completely. They are no longer in the front lines, they have long since retreated to the rear guard. From that position, their resentment terrorizes any formation of a new religious will. Millions of people are waiting for this new formation, and their yearnings remain unfulfilled.

Is our time not yet ripe? One might almost think it is not.

Some day we shall awaken magnificently in religion too.

Until then, let each man seek his God in his own way.

But we should allow the broad masses to worship their idols until we can give them a new God.

I take the Bible, and all evening long I read the simplest and greatest sermon that has ever been given to mankind: The Sermon on the Mount!

"Blessed are they who suffer persecution for the sake of justice, for theirs is the kingdom of heaven!"

6 November

My comrades love me. They help me, nay, they anticipate my every wish.

One mends my shoes, I give him the leather; he refuses to be paid for the work.

Another takes along my work uniform to wash it at home.

A third brings me two fat, red apples in the morning. He says he has so many.

Someone else comes to me and asks me who Nietzsche was.

They help me, I help them.

I live as a comrade among these plain, simple, strong men. They are all endlessly harried and poisoned. But the poison can be gotten rid of. We only have to make an effort and work.

They treat me like a peer now.

They all address me in the familiar form, and I address all of them in the familiar form. As we did out on the front lines, in the trenches. I feel at home in the pit.

This is what the Fatherland should be like some day. Everyone not equal, but all of us brothers.

In the evening, I sit with the other men. We talk, argue, fight, bitch. I bitch with them from the bottom of my heart.

A man must bitch every now and then, talk the resentment out of his soul.

I visit them at home, I play with their children, chat with their wives.

I tell them about my travels, I show them postcards and pictures.

When I walk through the streets, the children come and hold my hand.

10 November

Now I have many brothers. They are all like brothers to me.

Brothers of work! All who come from the same blood and bear a common destiny are brothers.

And we all have to bear the same destiny, we Germans. Why should we not all be brothers?

We have gone through so much misery together, that we cannot come apart.

I am nothing more and nothing less than all the others.

A young German! A fighter, a sufferer, who wants to overcome!

We must join together, we Germans!

For our final goods!

If we succeed in creating a new German type to show other nations, then we shall shape the coming millennium.

16 November

Now I am completely free!

The miracle is taking place within me: A new world is beginning.

The way lies open now. I have paved it by means of work.

We must all do redemptive work sooner or later, first with ourselves, then with others.

You must overcome your own life, then we shall be strong enough to shape the life of the era.

20 November

I sought in the mind and did not find the way.

We must conquer the mind.

I sought in work and did not find the way.

We must purify work.

And now the enigma solves itself.

The new law arises.

The law of work, which means fight, and the law of the mind, which is work. The synthesis of these three sets us free, mentally and physically.

Work as struggle, mind as work—that is our salvation!

My eye sees clearly! The way is free!

The birth within me!

My hardened hands begin to tremble.

29 November

I have trampled Ivan Vienurovsky to the ground:

In him I have conquered the Russian.

I have redeemed myself:

In me I free the German.

Now we both stand as relentless opponents, facing one another.

Armed to the teeth, for it is the ultimate struggle!

Pan-Slavism! Pan-Germanism!

Who shall win the future?

No, I am not an apostate. I believe in us, in Germany!

The Reich will come amid pain and suffering!

The world today has good reasons to despise that which

pretends to be Germany.

We believe in ourselves all the more powerfully.

We are here! We young men live, and we shall cross swords with all enemies of our kind, fighting for the future.

When we come to ourselves again, the world shall tremble before us.

The globe belongs to he who takes it.

2 December

My time here is over. I have learned all I could.

Tomorrow I shall leave for the Bavarian mines.

What drives me to move on? I do not know.

Perhaps I am drawn by the solitude of the mountains.

I say farewell to everyone. I have never experienced so much love and devotion.

You men threw me to the ground, and now you are my friends.

I shall never forget you!

10 December

Have I aged twenty years? Have I slept, dreamt? I do not recognize my Munich.

There is the train station, the Stachus, the Marienplatz, the Theatinerkirche, there is the broad, pompous Ludwigstrasse! There lies Schwabing, as it did a year ago, and yet everything is different.

I have become a new man. My eyes are refocused.

I hear the dear sounds of Munich. A young man passes by with a Schwabing girl.

Students come from the university, carrying books and brief-cases.

Most of them look thin, pale, and earnest.

Did I not notice this wretchedness in the past?

The stigma on the forehead of the German people?

A hungry, famished, freezing youth.

In the evening, I sit in a large room, among a thousand people, and I see him again, the man who awakened me.

Now he stands in the midst of a faithful community.

I barely recognize him. He looks greater, more resolute. A vaster, more concentrated strength emanates from his lips, his hands, an ocean of light flashes from two blue stars.

I sit amid all the others and I feel as if he were speaking to me personally.

He talks about the boon of work! What I suffered and endured, what I felt is framed in words here. My profession of faith! Here it gains shape.

Work as salvation! Not money, but work and struggle set us free, you and me, all of us, and we are all the Fatherland.

I am overcome by a profound peace. I feel an ocean of strength roaring through my soul.

Here young Germany stands up, the workers who shall forge the Reich. Now they are an anvil, but some day they shall be the hammer!

Here is my place!

I want to stand here when we have to fight to the finish.

We must all become mature. Minorities win out only when they are better than the majority.

I am surrounded by people whom I have never seen, and I am embarrassed as a child when tears steal into my eyes.

12 December

"Several weeks ago, I received a letter from Hertha Holk. She is studying at Wurtzburg and preparing for an examination."

"Why are you telling me this, Agnes Stahl?"

"Because I suspect that you have not yet gotten over her."

"You are wrong. I have.

"I struggled very hard, but I did manage to get over her.

"The drudgery down in the pit makes everything else so trivial. You barely get a chance to think about yourself.

"I loved Hertha Holk very much. I still love her and will always love her. But she was not a comrade who would go through thick and thin with me. I do not believe one ever finds such a person.

"In the end, we can rely only on ourselves.

"Hertha Holk cares about the new, but she is still stuck in her old prejudices, her old views—in short, she is stuck in the bourgeoisie, which is already outdated. She does not have the courage to be consistent.

"Very few people have that courage!

"Hers is a traditional character. She makes compromises, she cares more for her peace of mind than the struggle and the prospect of victory or defeat.

"She could not wait.

"She had no time for me."

"You are being unfair to her."

"No, I am not angry at her. I understand everything now.

"She was my destiny, which gave me the final push to break through.

"We must be grateful to the people who give us a chance to make sacrifices."

A pause.

"And now you want to go back into the pit?"

"Yes, I am happy down there, and I feel that many there need me."

The studio is bare and empty. A final ray of twilight steals through the high windows.

I often sat here with Hertha Holk.

13 December

I visit Richard.

He has gotten his doctorate in Heidelberg and is now working for a major publisher.

He tells me so many things pell-mell. About new art and spiritual expressive values.

I listen without thinking about it. He has changed greatly. I notice it now as I observe him. His face has gotten fat, and a commanding pair of horn-rimmed spectacles perch on his nose. His movements are self-assured, self-confident. But he seems embarrassed in front of me.

I soon take my leave.

He calls me "dear Michael" and accompanies me outside the house. "Well, so long!" he calls after me.

I slowly walk down the street.

Suddenly he comes running after me, grabs my hand, and whispers to me in extreme agitation:

"Michael, I envy you. I'm awful."

Suddenly, I lose all my resentment towards him. I press his hand tightly.

We go our separate ways.

15 December

I meet a Russian student at the Old Pinakothek. He tells me the shattering news of Vienurovsky's death.

He went back to Russia in July. In St. Petersburg, he devoted himself to secret revolutionary activities, establishing special groups and starting small conspiracies. The authorities had him under observation, and they arrested him in September. After two weeks' imprisonment, they had to let him go, since they could not prove anything against him. In early November, his name appeared frequently in the newspapers. He was feverishly working on the exposé of a huge government corruption scandal.

On November 23, early in the morning, they found him on the sofa in his room: He had been shot and killed. All indications pointed to murder.

They say there are no clues leading to the perpetrators.

A string snaps within me.

Ivan Vienurovsky! You did not deserve to end in this way.

I think of you with some melancholy.

Your destiny is the destiny of your nation.

Shot and killed! No trace of the perpetrators.

18 December

I spend my last day in Munich with Agnes Stahl. I have a great deal to tell her.

I feel that she understands me.

I had to pour out my heart to someone that day.

Only a woman can grasp this.

Now I have nothing more to say.

It is like a conclusion.

3 January

I work in the mines near Schliersee. I have found the right way here.

The mountains refresh me after work.

I love looking up at them.
The work is not hard. I am strong and healthy.
My comrades are good to me.
I live with a simple farmer and his wife.
The land emanates strength and beauty.
The mountains are unshakable.
Men and times grow old and die.
But the mountains remain the same.
Eternally old and eternally young.

7 January
The war awoke me from a deep sleep. It brought me to consciousness.

My mind tormented me and drove me to my catastrophe; it showed me depth and height.

Work redeemed me. It made me proud and free.

And now I have reshaped myself from these three things.

I have made myself the proud, free, conscious German who shall win the future.

Christ gave me a great deal—but not everything.
We must awaken Him anew within ourselves.
We can do so only with our own conscious strength.

The individual's life is not everything. It is not a thing in itself. We must overcome it and rise to a new, fruitful power.

So long as a man clings to life, he remains unfree.

10 January
I feel an urge for faraway places, but my love always returns to the mother earth of my homeland.

18 January
Dearest Mother,
Now, the worst is behind me. I am free. I have overcome the things that tormented and oppressed me, that made me cleave to the earth. I have spread my wings, and I am preparing them for the flight into the blue yonder.

I thank you for giving me life. Can you understand that I

sometimes resented you for it?

For life is worth living. What the weary and exhausted say is not true. We are not put into this world in order to suffer and die.

We have a mission to carry out here.

Some people feel the drive for this mission strongly, others more weakly.

This drive burned in me like a sacrificial fire. I had to act as I did. Now that I have overcome, I yearn to see your dear face again.

Why should we worry about what the future will bring? I look forward to it, solid and secure. I feel strong enough to fight on. We became men too quickly, for we witnessed and suffered more in our youth than any previous generation.

Have we not managed to get through it? We pulled through and we shall continue to pull through.

Struggle costs blood. But every drop of blood is a seed.

Nothing happens for nothing on this earth. Everything is a beginning, a consequence, or an end.

29 January

Today my landlady comes weeping into my room and begs me not to go into the pit tomorrow. She says she dreamed that I was killed by a rock.

I have a hard time calming her down.

Dreams are but shadows!

I cannot forget it.

But are we not always one with death in the pit?

I do not want to die as yet!

We must all make sacrifices!

* * * * *

Here ends Michael's diary.

Alexander Neumann, a mining trainee, writes to Fräulein Hertha Holk in Würtzburg on February 26:

Only now can I go along with your wish, as transmitted to me by Fräulein Agnes Stahl, and inform you of the details of the sudden and shattering death of Michael. Michael came to us in Schliersee in late December of last year to work in the mines here. He lived near me, and chance as well as mutual liking soon made us loyal comrades. I might almost say friends. You may know yourself how easily one could get to like that simple and yet so great person.

On the morning of that catastrophic day, January 30, we walked to work together as usual. The distance to the mine is not great, perhaps half an hour.

It was five a.m., and the shift began at six. The morning was cuttingly cold, it was freezing, and we walked through high snow.

Michael was earnest and quiet.

He did not joke as he usually did on the way to and from work.

Suddenly, he halted and asked me:

"Is there such a thing as a presentiment? I feel as if I ought to turn back."

Then he shouted, laughing:

"Oh, how silly! Dreams are but shadows!"

Shortly before six a.m. we descended. I worked next to him in the narrow tunnel. We lay on our backs and knocked down the coal. Once he shouted something at me, but I did not understand. Towards ten a.m. I went into the new tunnel to have breakfast. He wanted to finish the work he had begun.

Suddenly I heard a dribbling, something broke, then came a brief, but violent crash. I dashed into the tunnel. Michael was lying on the ground. I held the lantern in his face. His eyes were shut. I felt his heart, it was still beating, he was still breathing.

I called over a few comrades, and we brought him up. He opened his eyes very briefly and mumbled something that I could not understand. The mine physician came immediately.

A falling rock had hit Michael on the head, causing a brain hemorrage. He had only a few hours left to live.

We brought him to the nearest house and placed him on a bed. He was calm, barely moved, and sometimes he whispered, "I am tired, I want to sleep."

He lay like that for a long time, two or three hours. Towards noon, he opened his eyes wide and gazed at us, astonished and alien. He said very loud and audibly: "Mother!"

And then the agony began.

He was delirious with feverish fantasies. His body shook. He fought as if with invisible foes. Then he shouted in his agony:

"Ivan, you villain!"

Suddenly, he said very softly: "Workers!"

And then he began to whisper. We could barely understand anything now. An occasional fragment. I thought I heard the words "sacrifice" and "work, war!"

Then he became very calm. His face was transfigured by a smile, and he died with that smile.

It was four in the afternoon.

He was placed on a bier in his room. His face was not disfigured. There was coagulated blood only at his nose.

Thus he lay in flowers and wreaths.

On the third day, his mother came after I sent her a telegram. She was more composed than I had expected.

On the fourth day, we brought him to his final resting place. It was a clear, frosty winter afternoon.

A few students from Munich, several young painters, and Agnes Stahl, the Swiss sculptress, accompanied him to the grave. Miners carried him. He was buried as a worker, student, and soldier. His comrades called out, "A final good luck for the long trip!"

On his table, they found an uncompleted postcard to Matthias Grützer in Gelsenkirchen. Michael writes about being a pioneer of the new Reich and advises us not to despair. His drawer contained *Faust*, the Bible, Nietzsche's *Thus Spake Zarathustra*, and a journal.

Now you know everything.

There is one more thing I would like to mention. It gave me a certain amount of insight into the fate of our mutual friend and, beyond lament and grief, it helped me to understand the symbolism of his death and its meaning for the future. Several weeks ago, Michael's mother sent me his *Zarathustra* as a keepsake. It is an old, ragged copy. He carried it in his kit bag all through the war. In the evening, I enjoy leafing through it.

And there I found a passage that Michael underlined twice with a thick red pencil:

Many die too late and some too soon,
The teaching still sounds strange: Die at the proper time!

About the Translator

Joachim Neugroschel, born in Vienna, was twice awarded the Goethe House prize for translation. He is the noted and sought-after translator of Elias Canetti, Albert Speer, Georges Bataille, Sholem Aleichem, Hans-Jurgen Syberberg, Theodor Adorno, Jacques Ellul and Paul Celan, among many others. Mr. Neugroschel is also a much-published poet and essayist.

From *Amok Press:*

Apocalypse Culture

It's been 2,000 years since the death of Christ and the world is going mad. Born-again pornographers, totalitarian occultists and nihilist kids are united in their belief of an imminent global catastrophe. *Apocalypse Culture*—with 33 expert dispatches from the front lines of the American *Grand Guignol*—fixes its microscope on the tumors of mass delirium.

This grand exposé of the current fin de siècle nightmare includes interviews with necrophiliacs and lycanthropes, transcendental masochists and disciples of the obscenely obese. The psychotic nether regions of art, science and politics are explored, with special attention given to the imbroglios of cultic conspirators.

Thought crimes of a new generation of aesthetic terrorists . . . the Satanic directives of The Process cult . . . disintegrating UFOs with Dr. Wilhelm Reich and his spaceguns . . . self-mutilations and cavorting with carcasses by artists of the dark . . . all the data fit to print on the decomposition of modern society. Institutionalized schizophrenics talk back to television, and one claims the power to make *Today* show's Bryant Gumbel blink. *Apocalypse Culture* is extensively and unnervingly illustrated, with social analysis guaranteed to go beyond the pleasure principle. An invaluable cause-and-effect primer on the impending end times. With an eye-popping full-color cover by *Mondo New York*'s Joe Coleman.

Edited by Adam Parfrey.

Trade paperback edition available November, 1987.

Amok Catalogue Third Dispatch

The Amok mail order catalogue sells challenging, unconventional book titles which have found no place in the 1980s book retailer's scrupulously market-researched shelves.

The Third Dispatch features an amazing array of non-fiction titles essential to the devoted researcher, skeptic, believer, or merely curious. Crime, kitsch, control, occultism, alternative looks at graven-in-stone scientific and historical myths are among the eclectic array of topics offered. Said the *L.A. Weekly* of the Amok Catalogue, "Barnes and Noble eat your heart out!"

Amok's Second Dispatch is devoted to human imagination in print, drawing from the under-recognized realms of "noir" pulp writers, fringe Science Fiction, non-Occidental writings, Surrealists, Symbolists, as well as placing such literary eminences as Poe, Lewis Carroll, Nietzsche, Celine and Dostoevsky in a post-industrial context. Wrote J.G. Ballard, "It's an impressive collection, absolutely definitive in many ways ... The whole thing, in fact, is a wonderful conspectus of that other literature that exists light-years away from mainstream publishing and the respectable academic consensus that underpins all puffed-up reputations and assorted nonentities..."

The Second and Third Dispatch (the latter makes its debut in January, 1988) are available for $1.00 each from AMOK, P.O. Box 875112, Los Angeles, CA, 90087.

Look for the AMOK store in Los Angeles' Silverlake district which carries new and used books, and guerrilla videos for sale or rental.